OTHELLO AND
OTHER STORIES FROM SHAKESPEARE'S PLAYS

The *Oxford Progressive English Readers* series provides a wide range of reading for learners of English.

Each book in the series has been written to follow the strict guidelines of a syllabus, wordlist and structure list. The texts are graded according to these guidelines; Grade 1 at a 1,400 word level, Grade 2 at a 2,100 word level, Grade 3 at a 3,100 word level, Grade 4 at a 3,700 word level and Grade 5 at a 5,000 word level.

The latest methods of text analysis, using specially designed software, ensure that readability is carefully controlled at every level. Any new words which are vital to the mood and style of the story are explained within the text, and reoccur throughout for maximum reinforcement. New language items are also clarified by attractive illustrations.

Each book has a short section containing carefully graded exercises and controlled activities, which test both global and specific understanding.

# Othello
## and Other Stories
### from Shakespeare's Plays

**Edited by David Foulds**

1993
Hong Kong
**Oxford University Press**
**Oxford Singapore Tokyo**

Oxford University Press

Oxford   New York   Toronto
Kuala Lumpur   Singapore   Hong Kong   Tokyo
Delhi   Bombay   Calcutta   Madras   Karachi
Nairobi   Dar es Salaam   Cape Town
Melbourne   Auckland   Madrid

and associated companies in
Berlin   Ibadan

Oxford is a trade mark of Oxford University Press

First published 1993

Illustrated by Choy Man Yung

Syllabus designer: David Foulds

Text processing and analysis by Luxfield Consultants Ltd.

ISBN 0 19 585465 9

Printed in Hong Kong
Published by Oxford University Press (Hong Kong) Ltd
18/F Warwick House, Tong Chong Street, Quarry Bay, Hong Kong

Oxford
Progressive
English Readers

# CONTENTS

# OTHELLO

### A brave soldier

Brabantio, a rich Senator of Venice, had a beautiful daughter, the gentle Desdemona. She was so beautiful and rich that many men wanted to marry her, but she did not love any of the handsome and wealthy young men of     5
Venice. She thought that a man's character and mind were more important than his age or his appearance. She chose for her lover a foreigner — a Moor from North Africa, whom her father often invited to his house.

The noble Moor was a brave soldier. He had fought for     10
the Venetians in their wars against the Turks, and had become a general in the Venetian army. The State thought highly of his abilities, and trusted him. His name was Othello.

Othello was not a young man, but he was a very     15
interesting person. As a soldier he had travelled far, and fought in many different countries. Desdemona loved to hear him tell stories of his adventures. He would talk of the battles he had fought and the dangers he had faced on land and sea. He had been taken prisoner by the     20
enemy, and sold into slavery. Then he had escaped. He spoke of the strange things he had seen, the great deserts, mountains reaching right up into the clouds, savage people who ate the bodies of their enemies, and a race of people in Africa whose heads grew, not on their     25
shoulders, but in their chests. These traveller's tales greatly interested Desdemona. Whenever Othello visited the house, she would get her work done as quickly as possible so that she could sit down and listen to him.

One day, when he had been telling her about his life,     30
she told him that she wished to live the same kind of life

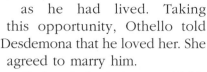

as he had lived. Taking this opportunity, Othello told Desdemona that he loved her. She agreed to marry him.

Brabantio had always told his daughter that she was free to choose her own husband, as she pleased. He had expected that, like all noble Venetian ladies, she would choose a man of high rank and of her own race and colour. But Desdemona loved the Moor. He was brave, strong, noble, an important man in the city, and an exciting man to be with. To her, the fact that he was an older man, and a foreigner was of no importance. The two decided to marry at once, in secret.

Their marriage did not remain a secret for long. Othello had an enemy called Iago, who was a soldier in the Venetian army. Iago had hoped to become a senior officer. Three of the most important people in the city had asked Othello to give him this position. But Othello had already chosen someone else — a man called Michael Cassio.

Iago had been given a much less important post, and he was very displeased about it. It seemed so unfair. He told his friend Roderigo that Othello had seen how well he had fought in Rhodes, Cyprus and other places. He could not understand why Othello liked Cassio better.

'Michael Cassio is a clever man,' said Iago, 'but he has never fought in a battle in his life!'

Iago hated Othello. He was angry that Othello had not made him a senior officer. He was jealous of Othello's military success. He had also heard people say that Othello had made love to his wife, Emilia.

Iago told Roderigo that he would serve in the army under Othello, and that he would appear to do his duty and be friendly. But he would only do these things for his own purposes. The truth was he wanted to make trouble for the Moor. 5

## The Turks in Cyprus

On the night of Othello's secret marriage to Desdemona, Iago and Roderigo went to Brabantio's house. They told him what had happened. Brabantio went mad with anger. He complained to the rulers of Venice about Othello. He 10 was a powerful man, and they had to listen to him.

At a meeting of the Senate, Brabantio accused the Moor of using witchcraft to make Desdemona marry him. He was very surprised that Desdemona had agreed to accept Othello as her husband. He believed that unless someone 15 had put some sort of magic spell on her, she would never have married him without asking for her father's consent first.

Othello, speaking simply and plainly, told the Senate what had happened. He admitted that he had married 20 Desdemona but denied that he had used any evil means to make her love him. Everyone believed him.

At that time the State of Venice urgently needed Othello's military assistance, and would not do anything against him. Even while the discussion about Othello's 25 marriage to Desdemona was taking place, news arrived about the Turkish fleet. It was on its way to attack the island of Cyprus, which in those days belonged to the Venetians. In this hour of danger, Othello was the only man the State trusted to lead the Venetian army against 30 the Turks.

Brabantio was urged to accept the marriage, as it had already taken place. He, however, insisted that Desdemona tell her story. If she said that she had married Othello willingly, he would withdraw his charges. 35

Desdemona then spoke to the Senate. She told them how much she loved and respected her father, but said she now had a greater duty to Othello, her lord and husband. In the same way, her mother had respected
5  Brabantio more than her own father.

Old Brabantio, unable to do anything else, gave his daughter to Othello, saying that he was glad he had no other children to disappoint him.

Once all these difficulties had been overcome, Othello
10  readily agreed to go to Cyprus and take command of the Venetian army there. Desdemona decided to go with her husband.

Othello had to leave immediately. He asked Iago, whom he thought was a friend, to take Desdemona safely
15  to Cyprus in another ship that would leave a few days later. Iago's wife, Emilia, would be her serving woman.

Brabantio, although he had accepted the marriage between Othello and Desdemona, was not happy about it. He warned Othello that Desdemona might deceive her husband as she had deceived her father.

**Iago's evil plan**

Shortly before Othello reached Cyprus, there was a violent
25  storm at sea. This caused great concern for Othello's safety, but it brought good news, too. The Governor of

Cyprus was informed that the same storm had destroyed almost all of the Turkish fleet.

As the Governor was standing by the shore, shouts were heard in the distance. The Venetian ship carrying Iago and Desdemona had arrived. It was a fast ship, and although it had not left Venice until after the others, it had reached Cyprus quickly. Othello's ship had been driven off course by the storm, but it arrived in Cyprus soon afterwards.

When they were on shore, Othello and Desdemona greeted each other tenderly. Saying that Desdemona would receive a warm welcome, Othello led his beautiful young wife to the Governor's castle. Among the welcoming party, watching their arrival, was Othello's Lieutenant, Michael Cassio.

Cassio was the friend of Othello and Desdemona. He was young and handsome. He had acted as a go-between for Othello and Desdemona, taking messages from one to the other before they had married. Othello was very thankful for his help, since he himself was not used to the kind of gentle conversation which pleased ladies. He had often sent Cassio to Brabantio's home, and it was no surprise that Desdemona looked on him as one of their closest friends. The courageous Othello, being of a serious nature, was happy that Desdemona and his friend, Cassio, could talk and laugh together.

Iago, who had come to Cyprus with Desdemona, was jealous of Cassio as much as he was jealous of Othello. He often made fun of Cassio as a man who, he said, was fit only for the company of ladies. Iago formed an evil plan for revenge. He would make trouble between Cassio, the Moor and Desdemona, and bring ruin to them all at one and the same time.

Iago was cunning. He understood the way people think. He knew that of all the pains which cause trouble between people, the pain of jealousy had the sharpest sting. He knew Othello had a 'free and open nature' which

could easily be influenced. By making Othello jealous of
Cassio, Iago would have his revenge.

The General's wedding, his arrival in Cyprus with his
lady, and the news of the destruction of the enemy fleet,
5   were all good reasons for a special holiday. Wine flowed
freely as everyone celebrated.

Cassio was Officer of the Guard. He had orders to keep
the Venetian soldiers from drinking too much, to avoid
any quarrels that would frighten the people of Cyprus.

10              **The drinking party**

That night Iago began his evil plans. He told Roderigo that
he thought Desdemona and Cassio were lovers. This made
Roderigo angry, because he had once loved Desdemona
himself and had wanted to marry her.

15   Iago told Roderigo that Cassio was a very quick-
tempered man. If Roderigo did something to make Cassio
angry, there would be a fight, and Iago could use this to
bring Cassio into disgrace. Roderigo, who now hated
Cassio as much as Iago did, agreed to help.

20   Later that evening Iago went to see Cassio, taking some
wine with him. He knew Cassio did not like drinking, but
Iago pretended he wanted to drink to the health of Othello
and Desdemona. He invited Cassio to drink with him. As
Cassio was the friend of the newly married couple, he
25   could not refuse.

Iago filled Cassio's cup with wine again and again. One
or two other people joined them, including the Governor
of Cyprus. They drank wine and sang songs together. The
more Cassio drank, the more he talked and the more
30   excited he became.

After a while Cassio had to leave the drinking party.
Iago then told the Governor that although Cassio was a
good soldier, he often got drunk in the evenings. At that
moment Roderigo walked by. Iago told him to go after
35   Cassio.

Soon there was the sound of someone shouting, 'Help! help!' A moment later Roderigo went running past, with Cassio, looking very angry, behind him. The Governor went to stop Cassio, but Cassio attacked him, too, and wounded him, and then tried to fight everyone else. Iago, who had started all this mischief, quietly told Roderigo to go and ring the castle bell. Othello heard the noise, and came with a group of gentlemen to see what was happening.

Othello questioned Cassio, who said nothing: he was too ashamed to reply. Iago seemed to be unwilling to say what Cassio had done. He pretended to make Cassio's offence seem small. He knew that if he did that, people would think he was protecting Cassio. Then they would imagine that what Cassio had done was really quite bad.

Othello could see that Cassio had behaved disgrace-fully. He said Cassio could no longer be his Lieutenant.

In this way, one part of Iago's plan had succeeded. His rival, Cassio, had been disgraced and removed from his position as a senior officer. But further use was to be made of the adventures of that night.

## Othello's jealousy

Cassio told Iago, whom he still thought was his friend, that he was sorry for his foolish behaviour. He knew he had made Othello angry. He wanted to get his position back, and he asked Iago what he should do.

Pretending to be friendly, Iago advised him to ask for Desdemona's help. She could plead his case to Othello, he said, and Othello would do anything that Desdemona asked him. Desdemona would be able to restore Cassio to the General's favour.

This was good advice, but it was given for a wicked purpose. If Cassio did as Iago had suggested, then Iago planned to make Othello ask himself why his wife was pleading for Cassio. Iago would then get Othello to believe that Desdemona had fallen in love with Cassio. This, Iago knew, would make Othello very unhappy.

Cassio followed Iago's advice. The next day he went to see Desdemona and asked for her help. Desdemona promised Cassio that she would do everything in her power to help him. She said that she would give Othello no peace until he pardoned Cassio.

Soon afterwards Desdemona spoke to Othello, asking him to forgive Cassio. She showed him how sorry poor Cassio was. She said it was unfair that Cassio should be given such a hard punishment. 'My lord,' she said, 'you know that before we were married, Cassio often came to talk to me about you. He always defended you when I was displeased with anything you had done. Now I am defending him from your displeasure. Really, I think this is a very little thing to ask. If ever I want to test your love, I will ask a much more serious favour.'

Othello could not say 'no' to his wife. He finally agreed to do as she wished.

Othello and Iago had entered the room together just as Cassio was leaving it after his conversation with Desdemona. Iago, full of cunning, said in a low voice, as if to himself, 'I do not like that.'

At the time Othello took little notice of what Iago had said, but when Desdemona had gone, he remembered it.

In this way, by his little remarks, cleverly planned questions, replies that were not as sincere as they seemed, and annoying reminders of Othello's own words, Iago gradually persuaded Othello to distrust the friendship between Cassio and Desdemona. Slowly Othello began to think there must be some meaning in all this, for he considered Iago an honest man. To himself he thought, 'Why did I marry? This honest creature, Iago, probably sees and knows more, much more, than he reveals.' However, he wanted to be sure. To Iago he said later, 'I know that my wife is beautiful, loves company and feasting, enjoys conversation, sings, plays, and dances well: but in someone who is of good character, there is nothing wrong with any of this. I must have proof before I think she is dishonest.'

Iago declared he had no proof of Desdemona's unfaithfulness. He only begged Othello to watch her behaviour closely and, he said, not to be jealous. At the same time he cunningly hinted that Venetian women, married to men of high rank, were often unfaithful to their husbands. He reminded Othello that Desdemona had deceived her father in marrying him. Othello was persuaded by this argument. If she had deceived her father, might she not deceive him, her husband?

Othello was full of grief when he thought about these things, but he refused to believe that Desdemona was false to him. However, he took Iago's advice. He delayed his pardon of Cassio in order to observe Cassio's behaviour with Desdemona.

In this way, another part of Iago's evil plan began to work. Othello was already unhappy, and Iago intended to trap Desdemona through her own goodness.

## The handkerchief

From then on the deceived Othello had no peace of mind. His work bored him. He no longer enjoyed fighting.

His heart seemed to have lost all that pride and ambition which are a soldier's strength. All his old joys left him. Sometimes he thought his wife was true to him, but sometimes he believed Iago.

5    One day he caught hold of Iago and demanded proof of Desdemona's guilt. Iago asked him if he knew his wife had a handkerchief with pictures of strawberries on it. Othello replied that it had been his first gift to her. Iago than said that he had seen Cassio using a handkerchief
10    that looked exactly the same.

This was a lie, but it made Othello very angry. Othello said that if Desdemona really had given Cassio her handkerchief, it must mean she loved him. He wanted revenge.

15    Iago made his wife, Emilia, who was Desdemona's servant, get him the handkerchief. Emilia did not know why he wanted it. She thought perhaps he was going
20    to have the pattern copied, so that he could give her a present just like it. In fact, Iago planned to put the handkerchief in Cassio's
25    room. When Cassio had the handkerchief, Iago would be able to 'prove' to Othello that Desdemona was unfaithful.

Later that day Othello asked Desdemona about the handkerchief. He said he wanted it. Poor Desdemona
30    could not find it. 'This is a great loss,' said Othello, angrily. 'An Egyptian woman, a witch who could read people's thoughts, gave that handkerchief to my mother. The witch told her that as long as she kept the handkerchief, it would make her gentle, and my father would love her; but, if
35    she lost it, or gave it away, then she would lose my father's love, too. He would hate her as much as he had once loved her.'

Desdemona was full of grief. She feared that having lost the handkerchief, she would also lose the love of her husband. Besides, Othello's anger worried her. To take his thoughts away from the handkerchief, she began to plead for Cassio once more. This made matters worse. Angrily, Othello left the room.

The gentle Desdemona began to suspect that her lord was jealous, but she only blamed herself for thinking badly of him. 'Men are not gods,' she said to herself. 'We must not expect the same respect from them when they are married, which they show us on our wedding day.'

Soon afterwards Othello discovered that Cassio did indeed have the handkerchief with pictures of strawberries on it. Cassio had found it in his room. Cassio said that he did not know how it came to be there, but Othello did not believe him. He decided that this was clear proof of Desdemona's guilt. Later he ordered Iago to kill Cassio. He said he would kill Desdemona himself.

## Othello's revenge

When Othello next saw Desdemona, he accused her of being unfaithful to him. He said he wished she had never been born. When he left her, Desdemona felt very tired and sad. She went to bed and cried herself to sleep.

As she was sleeping, Othello entered the room carrying a light. Moved by her beauty, he bent over her and kissed her. Desdemona woke up. Othello asked her if she had said her prayers. He told her to ask God to forgive her, because she was about to die.

Poor Desdemona was very frightened, and asked him what she had done wrong. She denied all the charges that Othello made against her. She said she had not given the handkerchief to Cassio, that she had never done anything to offend Othello, and that she had never loved Cassio more than as a friend. She said that if Cassio had the handkerchief, he must have found it somewhere.

But Othello thought that she was lying. He had decided that she must die before she could betray any other men.

Desdemona asked Othello to fetch Cassio so that he could be questioned. She thought Cassio would tell Othello the truth, and then Othello would realize what a mistake he had made. But when Othello told her that Iago had been sent to kill Cassio, she realized she had fallen into a trap. There was nothing she could do.

She begged Othello not to kill her, just to send her away, but he just pushed her roughly down onto the bed. As she struggled, she begged him again not to kill her then and there, but to wait for just one day, or, if not that, then just half an hour so she could pray to God. 'It is too late,' shouted Othello angrily. He pushed her head down into the pillow so that she could not breathe, and held her there until she stopped struggling, and was silent and still.

### 'Falsely murdered!'

Emilia knocked at the door. She seemed to be highly excited. She shouted to Othello that she wanted to speak to him. Othello let her in and asked her what was the matter.

'Cassio has just killed a young Venetian gentleman called Roderigo,' she said.

'Roderigo? What about Cassio. Wasn't Cassio killed, too?' Othello asked.

'No,' said Emilia.

Othello was puzzled, but just at that moment both he and Emilia heard a faint voice calling from the bed, 'Oh, falsely, falsely murdered!' it said.

Emilia recognized her lady's voice. She went to the bed and immediately realized that something was very wrong. 'Help, help,' she screamed. 'Oh lady, speak again. Sweet Desdemona! Oh sweet mistress, speak!'

'A guiltless death I die,' whispered Desdemona.

'Oh, what happened?' cried Emilia, who loved her young mistress. 'Who has done this to you?'

'Nobody,' whispered Desdemona weakly. 'I myself … Remember me to my kind lord. Oh …' Desdemona's head fell to one side. She was dead.                                    5

'What does she mean? How can she have been murdered?' said Othello.

'Who knows?' Emilia replied, but she looked at Othello suspiciously.

'You heard her say, herself, that it was not I.'        10

'She did say so — that is the truth.'

'Then she is a liar!' Othello shouted out. 'And like all liars she has gone to Hell. The truth is that I killed her!'

Othello tried to tell Emilia how wicked Desdemona had been, and that she was a false and unfaithful wife. Emilia   15 would not believe him, so he told her that her husband, Iago, knew all about it. He said that Iago had told him Desdemona had been unfaithful to him, and that she loved Michael Cassio.

'My husband told you that?' Emilia said, clearly       20 surprised.

'Yes, it was he who told me first. Your husband is an honest man. He hates wickedness.'

## Emilia speaks out

Emilia did not think that her husband could have said    25 anything bad about Desdemona. She refused to believe what Othello told her. She thought he was trying to blame Iago for Desdemona's death. She began to call out, very loudly, 'Help, help, oh help! The Moor has killed my mistress. Murder, murder!' Soon people came running to   30 see what was the matter, Iago among them.

'Oh, there you are, Iago,' said Emilia. 'Someone here is trying to blame you for a murder he has done. He claims you told him that his wife was unfaithful to him. Now you tell me it isn't true.'                                      35

'I told him what I thought, and only what he himself could see was the truth.'

'But did you ever say she was unfaithful to him?'

'I did.'

5 'Then you told a lie. A wicked lie. And did you say she was in love with Cassio?'

'Yes, with Cassio. Now, will you stop questioning me?'

'I will not. I have to know the truth. It seems the things you have been saying are the cause of this. Look, my
10 mistress is lying here, murdered in her bed.'

By then there were many people in the room. Until then they had not noticed Desdemona. They were shocked, and all started speaking at once. Many of them stared at Iago; they began to suspect he had played an
15 important part in this wicked deed.

'Are you mad?' Iago shouted at his wife angrily. 'Be quiet and go straight home.'

Emilia was not frightened of him. 'I know I ought to obey you,' she said, 'but not now that this has happened.
20 Let me speak.'

## The whole truth

Othello began to understand that he had made a dreadful mistake. He fell onto the bed, crying with anger and grief.

'Yes, it is good that you should lie there, roaring like
25 that,' Emilia shouted at him. 'You have killed the sweetest, most innocent young person in the world.'

'Oh no! She was unfaithful to me,' Othello shouted. He then noticed that one of the people in the room was Desdemona's uncle. Othello tried to explain to him that
30 he had killed Desdemona for a good reason, and mentioned the handkerchief.

'Oh God, oh heavenly God,' cried Emilia, who then understood what must have happened.

'Be quiet, woman,' whispered Iago, but she would not.
35 'I must tell the truth. I will not be silent. I don't care how many of you try to stop me, I will speak.'

'You would be wise to be quiet and go home,' said Iago. He spoke quietly and coldly, and pointed his dagger at her.

Emilia took no notice. She stared angrily at Othello.

'Oh you stupid Moor. I was the one who took that handkerchief. I gave it to my husband. I don't know why, but recently he has been asking me again and again to steal it for him.'

'You are lying!' shouted Iago.

'By heaven I am not lying.' Emilia replied. And she looked hard at Othello. 'You murderous animal. Why should a fool like you want to marry such a good, sweet woman?'

At that Othello lost control. He rushed at Iago. Some of the people in the room held him back, but Iago turned and ran out of the room. As he did so, he passed close by Emilia, and stabbed her. Emilia fell to the floor, dying. Her last wish was to be taken to the bed and placed beside the body of her poor young mistress.

Almost immediately after this, Cassio was brought into the room, bleeding. He was hurt as a result of fighting with Roderigo, but not badly enough to die from his wounds.

5     Cassio said that in Roderigo's pockets they had found some letters which proved the guilt of Iago. Othello asked Cassio how he had obtained Desdemona's handkerchief.

'I found it in my room,' answered Cassio, 'and Iago himself told me just now that he dropped it there for some
10     special purpose.'

Othello now knew the whole truth. He was shocked. Too late he saw how 'honest Iago' had led him to destroy his dear young wife, Desdemona, and to wrong Michael Cassio, his faithful Lieutenant.

15     Crying out that he had killed Desdemona, whom he had loved 'not wisely, but too well', he took out a dagger which was hidden in his clothing, and stabbed himself with it. He moved slowly towards Desdemona. 'I kissed you just before I killed you,' he said, 'and now, as I kill
20     myself, I die kissing you.' He bent over her, kissed her gently, and then fell onto the bed beside her, dead.

Those present were greatly shocked at what had taken place. Othello's noble nature was known to all, but he had allowed jealousy to ruin his good judgement. When
25     he was dead, his bravery and his noble character were remembered. Iago remained to be punished. An official left for Venice to report these sad events.

# TIMON OF ATHENS

### A generous man

Timon was a nobleman who lived in the city of Athens. His father left him a great fortune and he soon became well-known for his generosity. He loved to give presents to the people he knew, and he loved to help those in need. His house was open to everyone.

Traders and merchants were always coming to his house to sell him things. They never asked him to pay his bills immediately. They knew he was so rich that they had nothing to worry about. Poets and artists came to sell him their verses and their paintings. If Timon was pleased with their work, he would often give them gold.

Timon's fellow noblemen also freely enjoyed his generosity. He was always inviting them to feasts and parties. He often sent them presents for no reason at all except to make them happy. They all loved him.

Among those who kept Timon company, there were some who loved his money more than they loved him. Such a person was Ventidius, an important man, who had once borrowed a large amount of money from Timon to pay off a debt. Later, he gained a fortune at his father's death, but he did not bother to pay back what he owed to Timon. Others were less mean. They gave presents to Timon, but then they knew he would send them even richer gifts in return. There were also those who were not ashamed to ask him for presents by flattering him. They would speak very nicely to him, but in their hearts they would only be thinking of what he might give them.

The only person who was unlike Timon's daily companions was a sour and cynical philosopher called

Apemantus. He thought all people were foolish, and that they only did things for selfish reasons. He was never tired of speaking rudely and unpleasantly about people. However, no one paid much attention to him. Timon used
5   to scold him for his rudeness.

### Timon asks for help

As time went on, Timon's great wealth grew smaller because he spent his riches so freely on others. His steward, the chief servant in his house, warned him again
10  and again. Riches, Timon would reply, were meant to make people happy, and he enjoyed using his wealth to give pleasure to others. The steward, who loved his master sincerely, almost cried as he watched his master's property being so quickly wasted by false friends. He could see a
15  time coming when Timon would have nothing left. Then, he thought, Timon would lose all his friends, too.

Timon went on spending far more than his wealth allowed, and the day came when some merchants to whom he owed money began to demand payment
20  immediately. They had found out how little Timon really had. They wanted to be paid before the rest was spent or just given away.

Timon did not know why the merchants were so anxious. He just asked the steward to pay them anyway.
25  But then the day came when there was no money left at all, and no easy way of getting any.

At one time Timon had had many valuable possessions. He had owned houses and land. If he wanted money, all he needed to do was sell something. But now all his
30  property had been sold or promised to other people. He did not have enough to pay even half of the money he owed.

Timon was not worried when at last he understood. He had been very kind to many people. He supposed that he
35  had friends who would rush to help him as soon as they

heard of his difficulties. The steward told him that he had
appealed to a few of Timon's friends, but they had firmly
refused to give any help. Timon would not believe it. He
thought it was impossible that people could be so
ungrateful. So he made special requests to those he had     5
helped the most.

## A bad time to lend money

Lucullus was among the first to be asked. Timon had been
most generous to him in the past.

When one of Timon's servants, called Flaminius, arrived     10
at the house of Lucullus, the rich young nobleman
welcomed him eagerly. Lucullus thought that Timon had
sent him another present. He could

see Flaminius had something
hidden under his cloak, and
asked him what it was.

'Just an empty box, sir,'
Flaminius answered. 'My
good lord Timon urgently
needs some money to pay
his debts, and he is sure you
will help him with a loan.'

Lucullus could not believe
his ears.

'Oh dear. He is "sure" is he? That's unfortunate. You     25
know, your good lord Timon would be a fine gentleman
if he did not lead such a rich life. I have often mentioned
it to him at his dinners, and I've been back to his house
again for supper just to urge him to spend less. But he
never listens. Everyone has his faults, and Timon's fault is     30
that he is too generous to his friends.'

Lucullus then sent his own servants out of the room,
so he could speak to Flaminius in secret. 'Listen, honest
Flaminius,' he said. 'Your lord is a good, kind gentleman,
that's true; but you are wise enough to know that this is     35

a bad time to lend money. Now, here's a little money for
yourself. Just tell Timon that when you came here, I was
out.'

Flaminius was shocked. He threw the money in
5  Lucullus's face, and went off, full of anger.


## Nothing to spare

Lucius, another of Timon's friends, was in the town,
talking to some strangers he had just met. They were
telling him that Timon had no money left, and that
10  Lucullus had refused to help him.

'How shameful!' cried Lucius. 'How could Lucullus
refuse to help such a good lord. It is disgraceful.'

The strangers agreed.

'I expect you have heard,' Lucius continued, 'that I, too,
15  have received presents from Timon. Not as much as
Lucullus of course — just a little money, a few pieces of
silver, some jewels and small things like that. But if he
had come to me for help, I would never have refused.'

Just at that moment, another of Timon's servants came
20  along. When he saw Lucius, he stopped.

'Sir, my lord Timon has sent ...'

'What?' interrupted Lucius quickly, 'What has he sent?'
He turned to the strangers. 'I am so grateful to Lord Timon,
he is always sending me things. How shall I be able to
25  thank him, do you think?' Then he asked the servant again,
'So, what is it that he has he sent now?'

'He has sent me to ask if you could lend him some
money.'

Lucius smiled weakly. 'He must be playing a game with
30  me. I cannot believe he wants to borrow money. He has
so much.'

'He owes so much,' replied the servant.

Lucius thought carefully for a moment.

'How awfully selfish I have been,' he said. 'Just the
35  other day I put all my money into some small business I

was interested in. Oh, I am so sorry that I cannot lend
Timon anything at present. Please tell him that no one
could be sadder than myself at not being able to help such
an honourable gentleman.'

## The last to be asked

Another of Timon's servants went to the house of another
of Timon's friends, called Sempronius.

'So, he is sorry to trouble me,' Sempronius was saying
in answer to the servant's request. 'Well, he could have
tried Lucullus or Lucius — or even Ventidius: he is quite
rich now, since Timon helped him. All three of them owe
their wealth to Timon.'

'They have all been asked, sir, and they have all
refused.'

'Refused? Even Ventidius and Lucullus? How ungrateful
of them! And now he comes to me. I am the last.'

Sempronius walked about the room, thinking hard.
'Well that shows how little he loves me, doesn't it? Really
I am quite angry with him. I was one of the first to receive
a gift from him, you know, but I am the last he asks for
help. The trouble is, everyone in Athens will hear about
it. They will know he asked me last, and they will all laugh
at me because of it. People will think I am a fool if I help
him now. If he had sent to me first, I would have given
him three times as much as he needs, but now, as he has
made me look so foolish, I don't think it will be possible
for me to lend him anything.'

After that, Timon realized the truth about his friends.

## The final feast

From that day on, Timon's former friends carefully
avoided him. Timon's only visitors were the servants of
the merchants he had bought things from. They now
wanted their bills paid. Those who had lent him money

continued to ask him for payment. Now, instead of praise
and flattery, Timon received rudeness and insults. He
could not get in and out of his house without being
troubled by people demanding money.

5    Suddenly, unexpectedly, Timon's fortunes seemed to
change for the better. He invited all his former friends to
a great feast. 'So Timon was only making fun of us after
all, when he asked us to lend him money', they thought.
They sat down at the table, talking happily to one another.

10   They thought about the presents they might receive, and
they were looking forward to all the fine food that Timon
would place before them.

One covered dish after another was brought in. Clouds
of steam came from the dishes, and it looked as if the

15   feast would be a very good one. Speeches were made to
Timon, expressing regret that no one had been able to
help him: it was unfortunate, they said, that he had asked
for a loan just at a time when they themselves had had
no money. Timon replied, 'Do not worry my friends. I

20   have completely forgotten all about it.'

Pleased to be so easily forgiven, the guests eagerly
waited for the steaming dishes to be uncovered. Timon
offered a prayer to the gods. He asked the gods to give
each man what he deserved, and to give nothing to those
who were worth nothing. The
guests looked puzzled. Timon
soon showed what he meant.
'Uncover, dogs, and drink', he
cried as each man uncovered
the dish in front of him.
There was nothing in
each dish but hot water!

The guests were
amazed. Timon lifted
the cover from a large
bowl of hot water and
threw it in their faces.

He called them by insulting names, and drove them out
of his house. He threw dishes and dish covers after them.
They thought he had gone mad. In their hurry to escape
Timon's anger and scorn, they left their hats and cloaks
behind. Some of these even had jewels and valuable 5
ornaments (probably past gifts from Timon) pinned to
them.

That was the last feast Timon ever gave. He left Athens
and the company of his fellow men. Once he had seen
in them only good fellowship and kindness. Now he saw 10
only false flattery and greed. He could not bear their
company. He cursed the city of Athens and all the citizens,
young and old. He prayed to the gods to bring them all
to complete destruction. He went to live in the woods
outside Athens. He felt that the wild beasts were not so 15
cruel as men, and was content to live with them.

When Timon's servants discovered that he had left
them, they were sad. They would never forget Timon,
who had been the kindest of masters. 'In our hearts we
still serve our master together in sorrow,' said the steward, 20
as he looked at the emptiness around them. He shared
out what little money was left. He decided to look for
Timon himself, as he could not bear to think of him living
alone without food or shelter. He would have to search
hard, as no one knew where Lord Timon had gone. 25

## The General

At about this time Alcibiades, a general Timon knew well,
and who had once led the Athenian army against her
enemies, was forced to leave the city too. The reason was
this. One of Alcibiades' friends, an old soldier, had got 30
into a fight in Athens, and he had killed a man who had
insulted him. The Athenian Senate wanted to hang him
for this murder, but Alcibiades tried to save his life. He
tried to show the Senate how much the old soldier had
done for the city in times gone by. 35

As an Athenian, the man had fought in many wars, received many painful wounds, and lost much blood, all for the sake of the city. His strength and courage had helped Athens. Now, instead of fighting many of the city's
5  enemies, the man had fought just one of her citizens, and he had only done that because the man had insulted him. The Senate had been pleased to let the man shed his own life-blood for the city in the past, Alcibiades said; now that he had made a mistake and was in trouble, surely the
10  Senate could show just a little mercy.

The Senators would not change their minds. Showing mercy, they said, would only encourage other people to do even worse things. When the law was broken, criminals had to be punished. That was the only way
15  people could be made to respect the law. The Senators would not listen to anything Alcibiades said.

Alcibiades tried again and again to make them listen, and everyone got angrier and angrier. In the end the Senators were so displeased with Alcibiades that they
20  decided to punish him too. They forced him to go into exile. They made him leave Athens, his own city, and said he could never return.

In the forest, far from the city, Timon found shelter in a cave. He lived on what little food he could find in the
25  forest. Mostly he lived on the roots of plants, which he dug out of the ground with his bare hands.

One day, while digging for roots, he discovered a piece of gold. He dug a little deeper and soon found a large pile of treasure. There was enough gold there to do
30  anything. If he took it, Timon would be richer than he had ever been before. However, the sight of this bright gold reminded Timon that money made men greedy, selfish and mean. At first he felt the gold should remain there, where it would cause no trouble, but then another
35  idea came to him. Why not use it to punish greedy people for their wickedness? He kept a little to use if he needed it, but put most of it back.

Just as he had done this, he heard sounds of military music and soldiers marching. A band of soldiers arrived, led by Alcibiades. Alcibiades was now marching in revenge against the city of Athens. He needed money to pay his soldiers. At once, Timon gave Alcibiades some of the gold he had just found. He said that he hoped it would help to bring misery and ruin to the people of Athens, to rich and poor, men and women, young and old. Alcibiades asked Timon what he would like in return for all that money. Timon answered, 'The only thing I want is for all those people to be punished.' So Alcibiades left with the gold Timon had given him.

## A visitor

When it became known where Timon was living, the cynical philosopher Apemantus came to see him. He thought Timon might have become cynical, like himself, and he wanted to know if they shared the same views.

Apemantus thought all human beings were evil and he never had anything good to say about any of them. He took what he could from them without being in the least bit thankful. Timon, though he thought evil of men, did not want anything to do with them at all. He did not make use of anyone, either to help him live, or to keep him company. Even though Apemantus agreed with Timon's ideas about people, that did not make Timon like him. Timon thought the philosopher was just as bad as everyone else.

Apemantus urged Timon to use wicked people for his own purposes, instead of living such a lonely, uncomfortable life. That was the right way to treat people, he said. After all, in the past, they had taken everything from Timon, and given nothing back.

But Timon refused to return to the company of those he hated and scorned. He thought the philosopher was a coward for pretending to be a friend to those he could not love or respect. Apemantus felt that Timon was a fool for preferring to live alone in misery. Timon soon sent him away.

## The thieves

5  Later on, some thieves came into the forest. They were thin and hungry looking, and seemed to be very fierce.

'Where is all this gold you say Timon keeps here, then?' one of them asked. 'I doubt if there will be much — just a small part of what he used to have. It was the loss of

10  his gold and his friends that turned him mad with sadness, you remember, and caused him to come and live out here.'

'People say he still has plenty left,' another said.

'Well, let's catch him and see what happens. If he hates his gold, he will be happy to give us some. But what will

15  we do if he refuses to give it to us freely?'

At that point Timon came along, searching the forest for something to eat. When he saw the thieves, Timon knew what they were, but he was not frightened.

'How are you, thieves?' he said, in reply to their

20  greeting.

'We're soldiers, not thieves,' they answered.

'That's much the same,' said Timon.

'No, really. We aren't thieves. We are just poor men in need.'

25  'You certainly look poor. You look as if you need something to eat. But why should you be hungry? Look around you. There are plenty of roots and vegetables growing in the ground; there are a hundred good clean springs to drink from within a mile of here; there are

30  different kinds of fruit on the trees, and berries in the bushes. Nature is a generous housewife. She has all kinds of things for you to eat. Why should you be in need?'

The thieves thought this was very amusing. 'We can't live on grass, and berries, and water, like animals and

35  birds and fishes,' one of them said.

'No, and I suppose you think you can't live on the animals themselves, either,' Timon replied. 'What you want to feed on are the lives of men! But at least you do not pretend to be better than you are, and I am thankful to you for that. There are plenty more thieves who appear    5
to belong to respectable professions.'

## Everything's a thief

Timon took some gold coins from his clothes and threw them to the thieves. 'Here you are, you naughty thieves. Here's gold for you. Go and buy wine and drink    10
yourselves to death — that is the only way you will escape hanging!'

The thieves were down on their hands and knees immediately, looking for the gold coins. Timon kept on talking to them. At first they didn't pay    15
much attention to what he was saying, but after a while they began to listen. He began to talk about them, and in a very strange way.

'Don't put your trust in doctors,' Timon advised them. 'Doctors kill more people than you rob, and they take their money too. You do your thieving like good workmen. You shouldn't be ashamed of it. Listen, I'll tell you all about thieving. There are thieves all around us. The sun's a thief. He steals water from the sea. The moon's a thief. She takes her light from the sun. The sea's a thief. It steals the moon's strength to make its tides. The earth's a thief. It gets it's goodness from whatever is dropped onto it.    35

Everything's a thief. Nothing can be done about it. Laws, prison, whips, no matter how rough they might be, cannot stop thievery.'

The thieves looked at one another in complete silence.
5  Never in their lives had they heard anyone talking this way. Timon took out some more gold and threw it to them.

'So, come along, you thieves. Start robbing each other. Here's some more gold for you. Go ahead. Cut as many
10  throats as you like. Everyone that you meet is a thief, and no better than you. Go to Athens. Break into the shops. You can't really steal anything because everything has been stolen already. The people that lose what you take are all thieves themselves.'

15  'Well,' said the leader of the thieves, 'When someone like him persuades me to be a thief, I am almost persuaded not to be one!'

'He's only telling us this because he hates everyone,' said another. 'It's a trick. Really he is trying to make us
20  think we are failures in our own special profession.'

'I don't trust him. If he says we can do it, then I think I'll stop being a thief,' said a third.

The thieves picked up the gold coins and left, thoughtfully.

25  ## The steward

The steward, who had been searching for his master, came to the forest. Through love and loyalty, he had come to live with Timon as his servant. When he saw the sad change in his lord, he cried. Timon, formerly so richly
30  dressed, so full of life and laughter, was now in rags, sad and weary of life.

At first Timon would not believe that the steward was as loyal as he seemed. But when the steward plainly showed his affection and desire to stay and serve him,
35  Timon at last said he could see that there was still one

honest man left in the world. However, as he had no love
left in his heart for anyone, Timon would accept no
kindness even from his servant. He just offered the
steward some gold.

The steward made a last appeal. 'Oh, let me stay and   5
comfort you, my master', he cried. But Timon would not
agree, and the poor man left in sorrow.

Some days later, the steward returned with two of the
chief Senators of Athens. They had come to beg Timon
to save Athens. Alcibiades and his army were close to the   10
city, and looked as if they were going to attack it. They
might even burn it down. The Senators were very worried.
They said that there was no one in the city who could
lead the citizens in their struggle against Alcibiades.

Timon, when he was a young man, had once led the   15
armies of Athens successfully against the city's enemies.
Now they begged him to return. If he took command, he
would have full power to govern as he wished. He would
be honoured by all the citizens of Athens, and he would
receive great wealth.   20

These were the people who had been ungrateful to
Timon when he most needed their help. Now they
urgently needed his help!

They received a cold, heartless reply. Timon would not
help them even in the smallest way. 'If Alcibiades kills my   25
countrymen, let Alcibiades know that Timon does not
care.'

He pointed to a tree. He said to the Senators that if they
wanted to get rid of their troubles, they could 'come here,
and hang themselves.' The Senators left.   30

## Timon the man-hater

Alcibiades captured Athens, but did not burn the city or
kill all the citizens, as Timon had hoped. Instead he
listened to the Senators. They told him that many of the
men who forced him to go into exile had already died.   35

Most people in the city had done nothing to harm him. It would be unfair to kill them all.

Alcibiades promised to punish only the enemies of himself and Timon. He said none of the citizens of Athens
5  need be afraid of his soldiers because he would make sure that the soldiers obeyed the laws of the city.

Shortly before this, one of Alcibiades' soldiers had been walking through the woods where Timon lived. The soldier was looking for Timon, but instead he found a
10 grave. It was at the edge of the wood, by the sea shore. The soldier could see Timon's name on the tombstone. However, he could not read any of the other words that were written there, so he made a copy of them.

15     When Alcibiades had finished talking to the Senators, the soldier told him that he thought Timon was dead, and showed him the copy he had made of the writing on the
20 tombstone.

*Here lie I*
*Timon*
*Who hated everyone*
*Pass by & Curse me*
*If you wish*
*But do not stop to*
*Cry for me*

The words said
'Here lie I, Timon,
who hated everyone. Pass by and
curse me if you wish, but do not stop to cry for me.'
25  'These must be Timon's own words,' said Alcibiades thoughtfully. 'This is the way he thought in the later part of his life. He scorned our sorrow for his unhappiness. He thought nothing of the few tears we humans cried for him. Yet how cleverly this has ended! He has had his body
30 placed by the sea shore, where the great ocean's tears fall for ever on his simple grave. Noble Timon is dead, but he shall never be forgotten.'

# CORIOLANUS

## An angry crowd

In the early years of the Roman Republic, the city was
ruled by a council called the Senate. Its members were
called senators, and each year two of them were chosen
to be consuls. These were the highest officers of the State.    5
The senators and the consuls were aristocrats. They all
came from the oldest, richest, most respectable families in
the city — the patricians.

The common people — the plebians — had a say in
the government, too. Each year they chose officers called    10
tribunes to speak for them in the Senate. The duty of the
tribunes was to look after the interests of the plebians.
They had to protect them from being unjustly treated by
the patricians.

As time went by, the common people became more    15
powerful. They even took part in the choosing of the
consuls. Any patrician who wanted to be consul had to
win the approval of the people. If the plebians did not
like him, he could not become consul.

Naturally, the patricians were not pleased with this.    20
They thought they were much better than the plebians in
every way. They wanted to rule the city without giving
any thought to what the plebians liked or did not like.
The plebians, of course, suspected that the patricians
would rule the city for their own, selfish reasons, and do    25
nothing for them.

One year there was a terrible shortage of food. The
poor, hungry plebians blamed the patricians for the
problem. The patricians owned the corn stores, and the
people thought the patricians were saving the corn so that    30
they could sell it at a higher price, later. They said the
patricians were trying to make themselves richer in this

cruel way. They were especially angry with an aristocrat called Caius Martius.

One morning some of the citizens began to gather in the streets. They were hungry. Many of them called out 5 angrily to one another. They had sticks and clubs and other weapons in their hands. It looked as if there was going to be a riot. Gradually the citizens joined together to form a crowd in one of the small, open places of Rome.

'Listen to me!' shouted one of them, who seemed to be 10 their leader.

The rest quietened down and turned their faces to the speaker.

'Now, first of all: we would rather die than go on being hungry like this, wouldn't we? All agreed?'

15 'Agreed!' they all shouted.

'And we know that our worst enemy is Caius Martius!'

'Yes! We know it,' came the response.

'So we are going to kill him. If we kill him, we shall be able to get the corn we need at a fair price!'

20 'That's enough talk,' shouted one very loud voice from the back of the crowd. 'What we want is action. Come on, friends. Let's get started!'

## The proud aristocrat

The crowd, which was now beginning to look very 25 dangerous, roared in agreement.

'Just one word, good citizens,' called out another man. He was tall and thin, and older than most of the others.

'Good citizens?' asked the leader. 'Is that what you said? We are the poor citizens, that's who we are. The good 30 citizens are the patricians — good and fat!'

The crowd laughed, and the thin man looked uncomfortable.

'And how do they get so good and fat?' continued the leader. 'By keeping us poor and thin, that's how they do 35 it. They use our suffering to make themselves rich. Now, let's use our sticks to take revenge on them, before we all get so thin we look like sticks ourselves!'

The crowd roared with delight at their leader's humour. And the noisier they got, the braver they felt.

But the thin man spoke up again. He did not seem so certain as the others. 'Are you going to take revenge especially on Caius Martius?'

'Yes! yes!' they all shouted. 'He's the worst!'

'But have you thought about how much he has done for Rome?'

'Yes we have,' the leader replied, 'and if that were all, we'd speak well of him for it. But everything he has done has been done out of pride. You might believe he did those things for his country, but I can tell you he really did them to please that aristocratic mother of his, and to increase his pride in himself.'

'But you cannot blame him for his own nature. And you cannot say he is a greedy man,' argued the thin man.

'Well, if I cannot say he is greedy, there are plenty of other things I can say. He has so many faults ... '

The leader was interrupted by the sound of shouting in the distance.

'Listen — our brothers have started a riot on the other side of the city. Why are we standing about here, wasting our time talking?'

The crowd was just about to move, but at exactly that moment one of the senators, Menenius, came along.

Menenius came up to face the crowd. He was not afraid of them. This old man was a friend of Caius Martius, but he was also well liked by the people. He tried to persuade them to calm down. As they liked him, they listened.

Menenius told them the food shortage was not caused by men or by the Senate, which was really concerned for the good of everyone. The State and all its citizens, he said, needed each other.

To show this more clearly, he told them a story. There was a time, he said, when the other parts of the body

turned against the stomach. They said that it kept the food that came into it. It was lazy, it never joined with the other parts of the body in the work, and just left them to look after themselves. The stomach answered these
5  accusations, saying, 'Yes, it is true that I receive the food. But I do not keep it to myself. Instead I send it through the blood to make the body strong and keep all its parts alive. Through my services the whole body stays healthy. I only keep that part of the food which is useless to the
10  body as a whole.'

'The Senators of Rome are like this good stomach,' Menenius explained, 'and you are the angry arms and legs. The State, like the body, will suffer if it has members who don't agree with each other.'

15  The people received this story well — but just then Caius Martius himself came by. He began to scold the discontented citizens. He called them dogs. He blamed them for being stupid. He said he could never trust them, for they were always changing their minds. Hearing from
20  Menenius that they wanted corn at a cheap price, he scolded them for daring to demand this. He took out his sword and threatened them, and began to drive them away. Caius Martius believed that the people were rough and must be ruled very firmly. He also disliked their representatives, the tribunes. He thought they would cause trouble, and that they would weaken the Roman Republic.

## Caius Martius goes to war

Rome had some old enemies and rivals called the Volsces.
Their chief city was Corioli and their leader in previous
wars was Tullus Aufidius. He had been beaten by Caius
Martius, but he was a brave and skilful soldier all the same.    5
When the Volsces saw that the city of Rome was suffering
from a shortage of food and from political quarrels, they
got ready to attack it.

When the Roman Senate heard that the Volsces were
going to attack Rome, they immediately formed an army.    10
One of the two consuls for the year would lead it and be
its General. Caius Martius was appointed to be second in
command.

The two tribunes, who spoke for the common people,
were present when the Senate made this decision. They    15
hated Caius for his pride, and for the way he scorned the
people. They were surprised that such a proud man would
agree to serve under the Consul. They thought that Caius
was being cunning. 'If Rome wins, Caius will take all the
praise, but if the Roman army is defeated, he will blame    20
the consuls.'

The Volscian leaders heard of the Roman preparations
for war. They decided to divide their forces into two parts.
The larger part would be led by Tullus Aufidius against
the city of Rome. The smaller part would be left to defend    25
the city of Corioli.

The Roman soldiers marched out from Rome, leaving
behind them wives, mothers and sisters, who anxiously
waited to hear any news of the battle. The wife of
Caius Martius was very fearful and worried. However his    30
mother, Volumnia, like many women of early Rome,
thought more of honour than of safety. To her, Caius's
wife seemed weak because she showed her fear. But they
did not have to wait long before a friend brought them
some news. He said that the main Roman army had met    35
the Volscian army, and a great battle was taking place.

However, Caius Martius was not fighting in that battle. He had been sent with a part of the army to attack Corioli.

The news was true. At first Caius Martius and his men made an unsuccessful attack upon Corioli and were forced
5 to turn back. But Caius urged the Roman soldiers to attack again. Did they want to be known as cowards or courageous men? he asked them, and he led them in a second attack which drove the Volsces back into their city. Caius rushed into Corioli after his enemies, but none of
10 the Roman soldiers followed. The Volsces surrounded Caius and forced him back out, wounded and bleeding. Seeing his great bravery, his followers charged forward once more, and this time they all entered the city and captured it.

15 Caius Martius ordered a few men to guard Corioli to make sure the Volsces did not try to take it back. Then, although he was wounded, he hurried off with the rest to join the main Roman army a mile away. He arrived in time to join in the battle that was still being fought there. He
20 attacked the section of the Volscian army under Aufidius.

Caius and Aufidius fought, man to man. It was a long, hard fight, as both men were good soldiers, and they were both very brave. However, Caius was too strong for Aufidius, and slowly began to beat him back. Fortunately
25 for Aufidius, some of his followers came and rescued him, but they could do nothing else. The Volscian army was beaten and had to surrender.

The Romans treated their enemies with mercy. After the victory they gave back the city of Corioli to the Volsces.
30 But Aufidius hated the Romans, and most of all he hated Caius Martius, who had beaten him many times in battle. He decided to work against Caius Martius, and try to destroy him.

Through the courage and strength of Caius Martius, the
35 Romans had won a great victory. For this, and for his part in the capture of Corioli, they offered him most of the property that had been taken from the Volsces, but he said

he wanted nothing. The honour of serving Rome was enough for him. He was therefore given a special name. From then on Caius Martius became known as Caius Martius Coriolanus.

## The people's hero

The news of the Roman victory and of Coriolanus's bravery soon reached Rome. Everyone was pleased, except the tribunes. They were happy about the victory, but they were angry that Coriolanus had been so successful.

The tribunes watched Coriolanus returning to Rome in victory. They watched him being praised by his friends. They saw how even the common people cheered him, and they dared not show their displeasure. Privately, they feared he might be given the highest position in the State by becoming one of the consuls. If he did, they thought he would use his power to take away the rights of the people.

The tribunes were very worried about this. Their only hope was that his proud behaviour would cause his own defeat. They planned to make him angry so that he would start treating the public scornfully. If he did that, they were sure the people would turn against him.

Shortly after this, the Senate met for the election of the consuls. One of the out-going consuls, Cominius, suggested Coriolanus should be elected. He told the Senators about Coriolanus's bravery, his fine leadership, and his refusal to take personal rewards for his victories. The Senate were pleased to choose Coriolanus.

To complete the election, the new consul had to make a speech to the people in the market place and win their approval. Coriolanus did not want to do this. He said he was not a good speaker. But he was persuaded to appear in public. When he spoke, however, he did not even try to be persuasive. He spoke insultingly to the people who

asked him questions. In spite of this, the people readily accepted him as Consul. Most of the time they did not like Coriolanus as a man, but they loved him as a fighter, and as the winner of great victories for Rome. For the
5   moment, he was their hero.

The tribunes followed the people's decision. Later, when they heard complaints of Coriolanus's scornful manner, they tried to get the people to change their minds.

'Coriolanus has always been your enemy,' they
10  reminded them. 'As Consul, he will have even greater power to harm you. He will take away all your rights. It is still not too late to vote against him. Say, if you like, that we told you to vote for him, and it was to please us, your tribunes, that you did so.'

15   ## The people turn against Coriolanus

Coriolanus began his new duties as Consul. News came that the Volsces were planning another war. As Consul, Coriolanus was certainly the most suitable leader to meet this new danger. But while he and the other senators were
20  talking about what to do, the tribunes interrupted them. The people, they reported, had decided against the election of Coriolanus.

This unexpected change seemed to Coriolanus further proof of the foolishness of the ordinary people. He did
25  not try to hide his scorn for them and their tribunes. The tribunes in turn blamed Coriolanus for his proud behaviour and for his lack of concern for the people during the time they suffered from the shortage of food.

Menenius tried to calm both sides, but without success.
30  Both parties were very angry. One of the tribunes turned to Coriolanus. 'You speak of the people as if you were a god who has come to punish them, not as a man who is as weak as they are!' he exclaimed. The tribune said he would let the people know how scornfully Coriolanus had
35  spoken of them.

Coriolanus could only see danger to the State in allowing the people to play a part in the government of Rome. In his view, the Senate had to make a decision. It must take away the political power of the plebians. If not, everyone would suffer the results by letting foolish, ordinary people direct important matters of state. He spoke out against the people's rights. But the law said the people had those rights, and it was against the law to try to take them away.

This made the quarrel even worse. When Coriolanus began to talk of taking away the rights of the people, the tribunes at once demanded that he should be arrested for treason, as he had spoken against the laws of the State. Menenius and other wise senators could do nothing to calm the situation. A crowd of angry citizens crying, 'Down with him! Down with him!' gathered to attack Coriolanus. However, his friends managed to drive them away.

## Sent into exile

Menenius persuaded Coriolanus to go home, and then he went to talk to the crowd. He was a peace-loving man and could not understand Coriolanus's strong speeches against the people. Menenius spoke to them in a gentle, friendly way. He said that in spite of his faults, Coriolanus deserved much for his services to his country. He advised the tribunes to behave wisely. They could send for Coriolanus and give him time to answer the people who accused him, and make peace with them. The tribunes and the crowd agreed to follow Menenius's plan.

Volumnia, Coriolanus's mother, was a proud aristocrat. Like him, she did not agree with allowing the common people to have rights in the government. But she urged him to be milder in his answers to the crowd. When he was firmly settled as Consul, she said, then he could do as he wished.

Coriolanus, who respected his mother very much, accepted her advice. Menenius and a party of friends from the Senate came. They urged him to apologize to the people.

5   At this point Cominius brought news of an angry riot. The safety of Coriolanus, his family, his friends and the city was in danger. Coriolanus unwillingly agreed to face the people and answer their accusations carefully, even if he had to flatter them by saying good things about them
10  that he did not mean.

However, his change from rough to mild came too late. The jealous tribunes had been busy turning the people against him. They had prepared many traps to make him lose his temper and so speak scornfully to the people.
15  The citizens were advised to accuse Coriolanus of trying to be a tyrant and taking all the power of the State for himself, or of being a traitor against the State. The tribunes also made the people say that Coriolanus had secretly kept some of the property taken from the Volsces for himself.
20  So when Coriolanus addressed the people mildly, he did not receive the response he had hoped for.

Menenius as usual tried to show the people that they should pardon Coriolanus's roughness as being something natural in a soldier and leader. But the tribunes did not
25  want to make peace. One of them stepped forward and accused Coriolanus of being a traitor. Coriolanus replied that he was not. He shouted at the tribune. He said that he would not buy the people's mercy by flattering them.

This was exactly what the tribunes wanted to hear.
30  Coriolanus had insulted the people and the tribunes in public, and he had broken the law. The tribunes then pronounced sentence against Coriolanus in the name of the people. He was not allowed to live in Rome any longer, but had to go into exile. The crowd shouted in
35  support of this.

Coriolanus honoured the law and so he accepted this decision. Perhaps he also knew that the people of Rome would soon regret what they had done. Refusing to allow anyone to go with him into exile, he left the city alone after saying a sad goodbye to his family and friends.

For a while after that, there was peace in the city, and the tribunes felt pleased with their victory over their enemy.

## Coriolanus joins the Volsces

The peace did not last long. The Volsces soon heard of the exile of Coriolanus, who was the only Roman they really feared. They prepared to attack Rome once again. Moreover, Coriolanus, bitter at the thanklessness of his countrymen, decided to join the Volsces! He went to Antium, a Volscian city, to offer Aufidius his help.

Coriolanus entered Antium disguised as a beggar. His face was well covered. It would not do for the citizens of Antium to see him: he had killed too many of them, and their relatives.

Someone told him that Aufidius was holding a feast that day for many guests. Coriolanus reached the house and found his way into the outer rooms. The servants were surprised to see such a poor-looking person there.

'What do you want?' one of them asked. 'There's nothing for you here. Go away, please.'

'If they knew who I was,' thought Coriolanus, 'they would not have treated me any better than this. Probably worse!'

A second servant came along. 'Where have you come from?' he asked, looking at the ragged, dirty clothes Coriolanus was wearing. 'You're not supposed to be in here. The guard must be blind, letting people like you into the house. Get out!'

'Oh, get out of my way!' said Coriolanus impatiently.

'Get out of your way? You get out! Get out of the house!'

'Now you are making trouble for yourself,' said Coriolanus dangerously.

'Oh, what a brave one this is!' the second servant responded. 'Well, we shall soon see how brave you are, beggar! I'll get someone to talk to you straight away.'

'I'll go and fetch the master,' said the first servant, and
5   hurried off.

A few minutes Aufidius came over. 'So, where is this fellow?' he asked.

'Here, sir,' the second servant replied. 'I would have given him a good beating, sir, but I did not want the noise
10   to disturb your guests.'

Aufidius looked at the 'beggar'. He began to think that things might not be exactly as they appeared. 'Where are you from?' he asked.

Coriolanus said nothing.
15   'What do you want?'
No answer.
'What is your name?'
Still no answer.
Slowly Coriolanus
20   began to remove the
ragged clothing that
covered his head and
shoulders. 'If you do
not know me, now,'
25   he said, 'then I shall
have to give you my
name myself.'

'What is your name?'
Aufidius repeated his
30   question, but he was
staring at Coriolanus
if he could not believe
his eyes. What he was thinking seemed impossible.

'The answer will not please you, I think,' said
35   Coriolanus. 'My name is Caius Martius. I have done much
harm to you and all the citizens of Corioli, which is why
the Romans call me Coriolanus. That is the only reward I

have for all the pain I have suffered, all the danger I have been through, all the blood I have lost in the service of my thankless country.'

Coriolanus then went on to explain how the common people of Rome had forced him into exile. Now he wanted revenge against them. He offered to join Aufidius in a war against Rome. If Aufidius did not like this idea, he said, then he could kill him.

Aufidius was delighted that Coriolanus had come in friendship. He gave him command of half the army.

## A mother's persuasion

When the tribunes in Rome heard about this, they did not at first believe it. They punished the poor messenger for bringing such unpleasant news. But other messengers brought the same news. Menenius and Cominius pointed out to the tribunes the terrible results of their banishment of Coriolanus. The enemy had gained what Rome had lost — his skill and bravery. Rome was in danger. Now the citizens regretted their thoughtless action.

The Senate met, and they decided to try to persuade Coriolanus to come back. The common people seemed to forget that they once hated Coriolanus for scorning them. They, too, were ready to allow him back from exile.

Cominius went to Antium and begged Coriolanus to return to Rome, but he refused. The tribunes, whose unwise acts had resulted in his exile, felt too ashamed to beg him to come back. The Senators tried once more. Good old Menenius was sent. He found Coriolanus with Aufidius. With tears he urged Coriolanus to pardon his countrymen. Coriolanus would not listen. He stopped him while he was speaking and sent him away.

As a last hope, his mother, wife and little son were sent to him. It was indeed difficult for Coriolanus to harden his heart against them. He was afraid to see them in private in case he gave in to them.

Volumnia appealed to his soldier's sense of honour, 'Do you think it is honourable for a nobleman to remember for long the wrongs that others have done to him?' She warned him that if he fought against his own country, he
5 would be cursed for ever. If he would not return, then she begged him to at least to make peace between Rome and the Volsces.

Coriolanus could not refuse to listen to the combined appeals of his wife, his mother and his child. 'Oh, my
10 mother,' he exclaimed, 'you have won a happy victory for Rome!' Suddenly he remembered Aufidius, who was standing near him. How could he make an enemy of his new friend? 'Aufidius,' he said, turning to him, 'though I cannot make true wars, I will make a good peace. If you
15 were in my place, could you have refused your mother, or given her any less?'

Before he joined the Volscian leaders to arrange a peace, he parted from his family with this praise, 'Ladies, you deserve to have a temple built to you: all the swords
20 in Italy could not have made this peace.'

Aufidius knew that the peace was not yet made. At last, he saw a chance for revenge. His old enemy was in his hands.

## Aufidius takes revenge

25 In Rome the people waited anxiously to hear the news. The tribunes no longer felt glad of their victory over Coriolanus. They feared for their own lives. The people now saw that the tribunes were the cause of all their troubles. The tribunes not only lost their popularity, but
30 were also in danger of being put to death. Suddenly matters changed.

Welcome news arrived that Coriolanus had decided to make peace. Crowds followed the Senators to meet the returning ladies. Volumnia and Coriolanus's wife waited
35 eagerly for his peaceful home-coming.

But Aufidius was now ready for his revenge on his old enemy who had so often beaten him in battle. He was also jealous of the good name Coriolanus had made as a leader of the Volscian army. Secretly, he informed some of his followers that Coriolanus had decided to make peace to spare Rome. He hinted that Coriolanus wanted to keep the Volscians from their chance of a splendid victory. He had become a traitor to his new friends.

Coriolanus met the Volscian nobles. He told them of the happy ending of their quarrel with Rome. To his surprise, Aufidius accused him of betraying the Volscians because of a few tears from his wife and mother. Instead of answering calmly, Coriolanus, always a man of honour, answered angrily. He called Aufidius a liar. He said if he had his sword with him, he would cut the Volscian leader to pieces. There was great excitement. Only one of the nobles asked for calm, but no one listened to him. Aufidius and the rest of the Volscian nobles took out their daggers, and killed Coriolanus.

This then was the end of Coriolanus. He had none of the cunning and evil ways of Aufidius. Even the citizens of Corioli, against whom he once fought, said, 'He shall have a noble memory.' He was a brave soldier and a fearless leader, but it was mainly his own pride that ruined his life.

# JULIUS CAESAR

## The new hero

As Rome became more powerful and spread her rule over many countries, the rich aristocrats lost much of their love and pride for Rome itself. Instead of working for the good of the people, they divided into different parties, each under its own leader. These groups often fought against one another.

This story begins at a time in the history of Rome when Julius Caesar was the most powerful man in the State. Caesar and one other great leader, Pompey, had just fought a battle. Pompey had been defeated and killed. Caesar then returned victoriously to Rome.

Some people in Rome believed that, at that time, the rule of one able man who cared about the good of the people would have been best. However, there were many who did not share that view. They wanted to keep to the old form of government, in which Rome was ruled by the Senate.

When Julius Caesar entered Rome after his victory over Pompey, the people crowded the streets to honour, welcome and praise him as a victorious hero. They were, according to the custom, given a public holiday. Not long before, they had praised the many victories of Pompey, who had won large areas of land for Rome in the east. But now, soon forgetting Pompey's services, the people were gathering in the streets to greet their new hero, and Pompey's enemy, Julius Caesar.

As they gathered, they were met by two of the men who spoke for the ordinary people in the government — the tribunes. The tribunes scolded the idle people for forgetting their loyalty to Pompey, whom they had once followed. 'What hard hearts you cruel men of Rome have!' one of them said. 'Don't you remember how much you loved Pompey? When he returned to Rome from his victories, you used to climb to the roofs and onto the tops of walls and sit there all day patiently waiting to see him. Now you put on your best clothes, cover the streets with flowers, and honour the man who has killed him!'

The tribunes were afraid that Caesar might win the people's support and then take all the political power in Rome for himself. They were afraid he would become a tyrant. They did not want the citizens to seem too welcoming to Caesar, so they tried to stop them from gathering to greet him. Their words had little affect, though. The people of Rome thought Caesar was a great general, and they wanted to see him.

Caesar entered the city of Rome in a public procession, accompanied by the leading citizens. There was Mark Antony, Caesar's chief officer in his battles; there was Brutus, a leading Senator and his trusted friend. But there were also some who were jealous of Caesar's success and popularity. As the ancient custom was for Rome to be ruled by the Senate, it seemed a dangerous thing to allow one man alone to have too much power over the State, even if he was wise and loved Rome. So Caesar had enemies among the senators.

## The Ides of March

As the procession moved through the streets, a fortune-teller made his way out of the crowd towards Caesar. He called Caesar by name, and warned him twice to be especially careful on the day known as the Ides of March. But Caesar would not listen to him, saying, 'He is a dreamer.' So the procession continued.

Brutus left the procession because he was troubled by certain thoughts and feelings. He found himself alone with a Senator named Cassius. This man had long been a secret enemy of Caesar, although in public he pretended to honour him. As they talked together, Cassius soon discovered that Brutus was afraid the people might ask Caesar to be King of Rome. Although Brutus loved and honoured Caesar, he feared that, as King, Caesar might misuse his power. Seeing Brutus's fears, Cassius began to tell Brutus certain facts which he hoped would make him distrust Caesar even more, and doubt his ability as a leader.

He told Brutus how Caesar had challenged him one day to swim across the River Tiber. Cassius had jumped in straight away, fully dressed, calling to Caesar to follow. They had both swum strongly in the rough water at first, but before they reached the far side, Caesar lost his strength and was unable to continue. 'Help me, Cassius, I am sinking,' he cried out. He might have drowned, but Cassius rescued him. Then there was the time when Caesar was with the army in Spain. He caught a fever. Cassius saw him trembling, and white-faced. He cried out, 'Please bring me something to drink,' like a sick child. Cassius said he was amazed that such a weak man could now be the master of the whole world. He wanted Brutus to believe that Caesar was no better than most men and should therefore have no right to rule like a god over others.

Cassius said that no noble Roman could allow the Roman people to be the slaves of any single man, and his warnings increased Brutus's secret fears for the future of Rome. Brutus promised Cassius that he would consider what he had said. To himself, Brutus thought that he would rather be a simple farmer than a citizen of Rome if Caesar really did become all-powerful. They talked about this seriously for a long time.

## The crown

Meanwhile, loud shouts of praise from the citizens sounded in the distance, where public games were being held in Caesar's honour. Soon afterwards the procession, returning from these celebrations, moved past Brutus and Cassius. Caesar had a sick, excited expression on his face, and most of the others with him seemed to be quite worried. 5

Caesar saw Cassius watching him. He turned to his friend, Mark Antony.

'Let me have fat men around me,' he said. 'The sort of people who sleep well at night. That Cassius has a thin, hungry look about him. He thinks too much. Men like 10 him are dangerous.'

'Oh, there is no need to fear him, Caesar,' Antony replied. 'He's not dangerous. He is a noble Roman, and he respects you.'

'Well, I wish he were fatter,' Caesar replied. 'Of course, 15 I am not afraid of him, but if I were afraid, I don't know anyone I would fear more than Cassius. He reads a great deal, you know. He watches everything. He understands exactly what people are thinking. And he is much too serious. He never goes to the theatre, as you do, Antony. 20 He never enjoys listening to music. He hardly ever smiles, and when he does, you can see he is surprised with himself for finding anything to smile about. But the worst thing about people like him, Antony, is that they are never happy when they meet people greater than themselves. 25 That is why they are so dangerous.'

Antony was about to say something, but Caesar quickly added, 'Of course I am only speaking about what a careful man should fear, not what I fear myself. After all, I am Caesar. Now, tell me what you think of him — but first 30 come over to my right; I am a little deaf in my left ear.'

As the procession passed by, Brutus caught the cloak of one of the Senators and pulled him aside. 'What has been happening, Casca?' he asked. 'Why does Caesar look so sad?' 35

'Oh, it's nothing very interesting,' Casca replied. 'Mark Antony offered Caesar a crown. He did it three times.

Each time Caesar refused it, but I don't think he really wanted to. The people loved him for refusing, of course.

5 Each time they cheered and clapped and threw their hats into the air. And then Caesar fell to the ground in a faint.'

'That's quite possible,' said Brutus. 'He suffers from the falling-sickness from time to time.

'When he came to himself again,' continued Casca, 'he
10 said if had done anything wrong, he hoped the people would excuse him because of his sickness. Three or four women standing near me cried out, 'Oh, the poor man,' and forgave him with all their hearts. But there is no need to take any notice of that. If Caesar had stabbed their
15 mothers, they would have forgiven him just as much!'

'And after that, he came away?'

'That's right.'

Casca's account of the offering of the crown made Brutus distrust Caesar's ambition even more.

20 **Strange times**

After the three had separated and gone to their homes, Cassius went a step further in his plan to make Brutus suspicious of Caesar's ambitions. He sent some letters to Brutus which looked as if they came from several writers.
25 All hinted at how the people of Rome looked to Brutus for protection against Caesar, who they thought was an enemy of Rome.

Later, that night, there was a terrible storm. Another Senator, Cicero, was hurrying home through the dark streets when he met Casca, looking quite frightened and carrying a sword.

'Why, what is the matter, Casca?' he asked. 'Why are you so breathless, and why are you staring about like that?' 5

'Doesn't it frighten you?' replied Casca, 'Oh, I have seen terrible storms before, but never one as bad as this, my friend. I actually saw fire dropping down from the sky just now. There is a riot in Heaven. The gods are at war, I tell you; or else they are so angry with the world they want to destroy it.'

Cicero was amused at Casca's fright. He thought a storm was just a storm. 'Have you seen any other strange things?' he asked. He enjoyed listening to Casca's tales, even if he didn't believe in them.

'I have!' Casca had much to tell. 'I saw one of our slaves hold up his left hand. It burst into flames and burnt as bright as twenty torches joined together, and yet he felt no pain. His skin was not hurt at all. And then, as I was walking past the Capitol, I saw a lion. It stared 30 at me, and went on. I have not put my sword down since. And after that I came across a crowd of women. There must have been a hundred or more of them — all terrified. They said they had seen men covered in flames, walking up and down the streets. And yesterday, at noon, someone 35 saw an owl in the market place. Now you never see owls, which are night birds, in the middle of the day.'

'I am sure there must be some natural explanation.'

'No, Cicero. When so many strange things occur all at once, it must mean something awful is going to happen.'

'Well, these are certainly amazing times we live in,' Cicero replied. 'But people often put a special meaning on things, which have nothing to do with the things themselves.' Then, changing the subject, he asked 'Is Caesar going to the Capitol tomorrow?'

'Yes. I heard him ask Antony to tell you to meet him there.'

'Good night then, Casca,' Cicero replied. 'This is no weather to be walking about in.'


## Caesar's slaves

A moment later Cassius came along. He was enjoying the storm. 'This dreadful night, in which the world seems to be being turned upside down, reminds me of a man, Casca,' he said. 'He is just an ordinary man, like you and me, but his power has become enormous and quite terrifying.'

'You mean Caesar, I think. Yes, I have heard that tomorrow the Senators plan to make him King.'

'If they do, we shall all become Caesar's slaves.' Cassius put his hand on his dagger. 'If you are right, Casca, I know where this will go. Cassius will save Cassius from slavery. The gods send things like this to make the weak strong, so they can overcome tyrants, and prisons, and chains.' Cassius looked closely at Casca, with a very serious expression on his face. Then he added, 'But perhaps I have said too much. Perhaps I am speaking to a man who is glad to be a slave of Caesar's!'

'You are speaking to Casca. I am as worried as you are about Caesar's power.'

The two men shook hands. They agreed to work together against Caesar's ambition. Then Cassius told Casca that some of the noblest senators had agreed to a

plan to solve the problem of Caesar's power, and Casca
agreed to join them. They were going to do something
that would be honourable, but dangerous and most
terrible, said Cassius. They were plotting to murder Julius
Caesar.                                                    5

## An honourable leader

The plotters wanted Brutus to be the leader of the plot
against Caesar. Brutus had great influence and he was
generally respected for his good character. He was a man
of honour. If the noble Brutus turned against Caesar, his    10
own friend, then people would surely think there must be
a very good reason for it. They would think the plot to
kill Caesar was just.

That same night, the night before the Ides of March,
Brutus could not sleep. He was disturbed by mixed         15
feelings and thoughts. It was true that Caesar was his
friend. But Caesar was likely to become a danger to the
State. Would it be better to kill a friend before that friend
put an end to the old government of Rome and took away
the rights of the people? He remembered that Caesar had    20
seemed sad when he refused the crown that Antony had
offered, but happy to please the people. If the people
wanted him to be King, then he would be willing to be
crowned. After that everyone would have to obey Caesar,
and they would all lose their freedom. The only way to     25
prevent that was by killing him.

As Brutus was thinking about these things, his servant
brought him notes which he had found by the window.
These were the letters prepared by Cassius. Brutus thought
they came from ordinary citizens. It seemed that these     30
proved how the people depended upon him to save
Rome.

It was after midnight. Brutus was still not sure whether
to kill Caesar or not when Cassius and his friends came
secretly to see him. Cassius asked Brutus to think of his   35

duty to the people of Rome. Finally Brutus agreed to join them. The details of the plot were then arranged. Someone suggested that Mark Antony, Caesar's chief General, should also be killed. But Brutus decided, against Cassius'
5   advice, to spare Mark Antony. To Brutus, Antony was not dangerous, for he was just a follower of Caesar's. Cassius, who was a wiser judge of character than Brutus, said that Antony was a very clever man who might later prove troublesome to them. In the end, Cassius unwillingly
10  agreed to Brutus's decision.

Decius, one of the plotters, said he would visit Caesar to make sure he would be at the Capitol the next day.

Portia, Brutus's loving and loyal wife, noticed how worried her husband had been since the previous
15  evening. Late that night she woke up and noticed Brutus had left the room. She heard him talking with several people, and became very worried about him. When the visitors left, she went to Brutus. She begged him to tell her the cause of his worry. Had she not, as his wife, a
20  right to share his secret? Brutus was about to reveal his worries to her when a visitor arrived. This was a man sent by Cassius. Brutus then promised Portia that he would tell her everything later.

### Terrible dreams

25  That night too, Caesar and his wife, Calpurnia, had a disturbed sleep. Calpurnia was frightened by her dreams. They seemed to be a warning her about the future. She tried to stop Caesar appearing in public the following day. But Caesar did not take his wife's fears seriously. 'Cowards
30  die many times before their deaths,' he said, 'but the brave die only once.'

Then a message was sent to him by the fortune-tellers. They announced that the day was not a good one for Caesar to meet the Senate. He was about to tell Calpurnia
35  he would remain at home for her sake when Decius, as planned, arrived.

Caesar told Decius about Calpurnia's dream — how she had seen fountains of blood pouring out of Caesar's statue, and how many smiling Romans came to wash their hands in the blood. To Calpurnia this was a sign that Caesar would die. But Decius cunningly suggested another meaning. He said that so many smiling Romans washing their hands in Caesar's blood meant that great Rome would take new life from him. Cleverly he added that the Senate had decided to offer Caesar the crown on that day. That was enough for Caesar. He decided he would go to the Capitol.

Some of Cassius's group, pretending to be loyal friends, arrived. Caesar was pleased that they had gathered to accompany him to the Capitol. And so he left with the men who meant to take his life.

Meanwhile, some talk about the plot had become known. A man named Artemidorus knew that there would be times of trouble for Rome if Caesar died suddenly. He wrote a letter to warn Caesar. In his letter he named the chief plotters and warned that they were united in their decision to murder him. Then he waited in the street to hand his letter to Caesar as he passed.

As Caesar went by, Artemidorus came forward and held up the letter. Decius immediately pushed another paper in front of it. So Caesar never read the warning.

## The murder of Caesar

At the Capitol, one of the plotters called Mark Antony over to talk to him. Another asked Caesar to let a senator who had been sent away in exile return to Rome. As Caesar was answering this request, the plotters moved closer around him. Then Casca, followed by the rest, rushed forward and stabbed Caesar to death. Each man had to strike him. As Brutus stabbed him, Caesar fell to the ground. He cried out, 'Even you, Brutus?' And then he died.

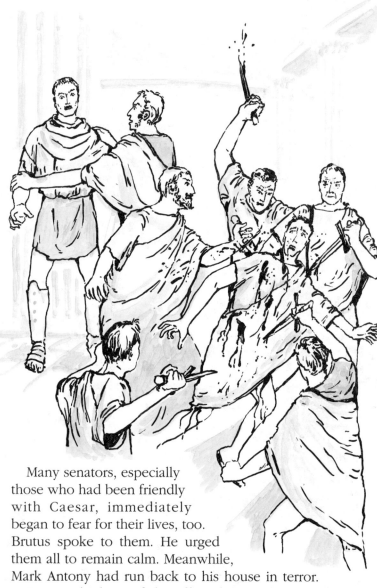

Many senators, especially
those who had been friendly
with Caesar, immediately
began to fear for their lives, too.
5  Brutus spoke to them. He urged
them all to remain calm. Meanwhile,
Mark Antony had run back to his house in terror.

Brutus, thinking of the effect the murder would have
upon the public, told his fellow plotters to go at once to
10  the market place to calm the people's fears. They were to
show the people the reasons for the murder, in order to
win their support.

Just then a servant brought a message from Antony, who asked for a promise of his safety. He said that he was willing to accept Caesar's murder if the plotters could show good reasons for it. Brutus returned a promise of safety and so Antony came to talk to the plotters. Being Caesar's friend, he boldly offered to be killed by their daggers so that he could fall with Caesar. But Brutus assured him of his safety and their friendship. Then Antony shook hands with each of the plotters, saying that he would remain friends with them all if they could tell him why Caesar was dangerous.

Brutus said he would allow Antony to speak to the people during the funeral ceremonies for Caesar. Cassius, who did not trust Antony, warned Brutus against giving permission. But Brutus replied that he would speak to the people first and give reasons for their act. He made Antony promise not to speak badly of the plotters.

Once Antony was alone, however, he showed his true feelings about the murderers. Looking at the body of his friend, he asked to be forgiven for his gentle behaviour towards them, and added that Caesar was one of the noblest men that ever lived. Then he foretold that misery and civil wars between Roman and Roman were sure to follow.

He did more. He secretly sent a message to young Octavius Caesar, Julius Caesar's nephew, telling him what had happened. He urged Octavius to be prepared for action and to have an army ready. Octavius was not far from Rome. In spite of his youth, he was known for being a great soldier.

## Funeral speeches

The body of Caesar was taken to the Forum — the Roman market place. There was a large crowd of people there, waiting to see what was happening. Before the body arrived, Brutus spoke to them, explaining why he had joined the others to kill his friend Caesar.

'If there is anyone here who was a dear friend of Caesar's,' he said, 'then I say to that man that Brutus was no less a friend to Caesar. The reason why I rose against Caesar was not because I loved Caesar less, but because I loved Rome more.

'Which would you prefer? Caesar alive, and yourselves dying as slaves? My countrymen, as Caesar loved me, I weep for him: as Caesar was fortunate, I am happy for him: as Caesar was courageous, I honour him: as Caesar was ambitious, I killed him. I give him my tears for his love, my joy for his fortune, my honour for his courage, and I give him death for his ambition.

'Is there anyone here who wants to be a slave? If there is, he should speak up, for I have offended him. Is there anyone here who does not want to be a Roman? If there is, he should speak up, for I have offended him. Is there anyone here who does not love his country? If there is, he should speak up, for I have offended him. I wait for a reply.'

The crowd was silent. Then one or two people shouted out, 'There's no one, Brutus, no one.'

'Then I have offended no one.'

The people cheered when Brutus ended his speech.

Then Antony came with others bearing Caesar's body. Brutus left the Forum, but before he went he urged the people to listen to Antony.

Brutus had tried to win the crowd by giving reasons for what had been done. Antony wisely appealed to their feelings, not to their minds. Though they were at first against him, he slowly gained control of their hearts. Brutus had told them Caesar was ambitious. Antony reminded them that Caesar had spent money on the poor and the citizens of Rome, not on himself. He had even refused the crown offered to him three times, as they had seen for themselves.

'Was that ambition?' Antony asked. 'Yet Brutus says he was ambitious. Well, Brutus is an honourable man, so you should pay attention to what he says.'

Antony's speech began to move all those who were listening. After a while they believed Antony more, and the honourable Brutus less.

To prove that Caesar was their friend, Antony told them about Caesar's will. He said that if the people read this will, they would feel sorry that Caesar was dead. By now the citizens were angry with the plotters.

Then he showed them the body, pointing to the wounds made by the daggers, and described how cruelly Caesar had been killed. The unkindest cut of all, he said, was the blow struck by Brutus, for Caesar had loved Brutus dearly.

The excited crowd was now full of anger. Then Antony told them about the contents of the will, in which Caesar had written down what he wanted to happen after he died. Caesar had left each citizen of Rome a gift of money. His private palace and all his gardens were to become public places, so that they and their children could enjoy themselves in their free time. This moved the already angry crowd to violent action. A riot began.

## The battle of Philippi

The people rushed away in all directions. They wanted to kill the murderers of Julius Caesar and burn down their houses. A harmless poet, who unfortunately had the same name as one of the plotters, Cinna, was torn to pieces, although he repeated he was a poet, not the plotter. Brutus and Cassius were warned in time, and they escaped from the city, riding like madmen through the gates of Rome.

As they left, Octavius Caesar, with his followers, entered by another gate. Together, he and Antony took control of the situation. They ordered the death of every important person who might challenge their power. When they had made themselves masters of Rome, they gathered forces to attack the armies of Brutus and Cassius. Caesar's death was meant to prevent a tyrant from ruling instead of the Senate, but it had brought terror to Rome.

5    Brutus and Cassius, in the meantime, waited in Macedonia with their armies, expecting an attack by Antony and Octavius. They had a fierce quarrel. Brutus needed gold to buy food for his soldiers, but he would not get it by unjust means, since he was a man of honour.

10    He had murdered Caesar in order to prevent tyranny and injustice! Cassius, however, was ready to use any means to obtain the money. Moreover, Brutus was a great thinker, not a man of action like Cassius. He kept making the wrong decisions, not depending on the wiser judgement

15    of Cassius. Yet Cassius allowed Brutus to have his way because he respected Brutus for his noble qualities and thought him the greater man.

Finally the armies of both parties met on the plains of Philippi in Macedonia. Brutus, hoping to avoid a war, tried

20    to arrange peace talks with the enemy leaders, but he failed. The battle began.

Before long the forces of Cassius were losing. They needed help from Brutus. Making yet another mistake of judgement, Brutus did not send help to Cassius, but put

25    his men into action against the soldiers of Octavius. Cassius, beaten by Antony, killed himself to avoid being taken back to Rome in shame as Antony's prisoner.

Brutus was doing well against Octavius until Antony's men came on the scene of the battle. Then, seeing there

30    was no longer any hope of victory left, Brutus, like Cassius, put an end to his life.

Perhaps Brutus came to realize, too late, that killing Caesar had not helped the people as he had intended. Antony looked at his body and said these moving words

35    of praise:

'This was the noblest Roman of them all.'

# ANTONY AND CLEOPATRA

## The foolish General

In a room in the palace of Cleopatra, Queen of Egypt, two Roman officers were talking quietly. Their names were Philo and Demetrius. They were both in the army of the great General, Antony, who at that time was one of the three leaders of the Roman world. Demetrius had only just arrived in Egypt, so Philo was telling him what had been happening.

'Our General is going too far in his love for the Egyptian Queen,' he was saying. 'Don't you remember how those good eyes of his were always bright with the joy of battle? Well, now those eyes are only bright when they look at his mistress. And that great Roman heart of his, which was sometimes so full of courage that it almost burst, now serves the Queen of Egypt.'

Demetrius was about to ask a question, but at that moment the room began to fill with people. Cleopatra came in with all her servants, courtiers and friends, Antony among them.

Cleopatra was standing in the middle of the room, with Antony quite close to her. She turned to him, with a mischievous look on her face. 'How much do you love me, then?' she asked. 'If you really love me, as you say you do, tell me how much.' She spoke loudly enough for everyone to hear.

'If I could tell you how much, then my love would be far too little,' Antony replied.

All the courtiers smiled. They waited to hear what would be said next.

'Well,' said Cleopatra, 'if you only loved me half as much as you say you do, how much love would that be?'

'We would have to find a new world to live in, and a new heaven, too. There is not enough room in this whole universe for even part of the love I have for Cleopatra!'

## Messengers from Rome

Philo looked at Demetrius and was about to say something when a servant hurried past. The servant went straight to Antony and knelt down in front of him.

15 'Some messengers have arrived with news from Rome, my good lord,' he said.

'Not now,' said Antony impatiently.

'Let us hear them, Antony,' interrupted Cleopatra. 'Perhaps your good wife, Fulvia, is angry with you, or

20 perhaps young Caesar has some important orders for you. They will say you must do this or that, or Caesar will punish you if you disobey.'

'My love?' Antony seemed surprised.

'I said "perhaps", but I think it must be certain,'

25 Cleopatra continued. 'This news will be that you must not stay here any longer. Caesar says you must leave Egypt. Or Fulvia says so — or both of them! So, let us hear what news the messengers have brought.'

Antony began to look uncomfortable.

30 'You are blushing, Antony. I see your blood is still loyal to Caesar. Or else your red cheek shows how ashamed you are when sharp-tongued Fulvia scolds you! Tell the messengers to come in. Let's hear the news from Rome!'

'Oh, Rome! I hope Rome falls into the River Tiber and

35 is washed away,' said Antony. 'It doesn't matter to me,

even, if this great wide Roman world falls to pieces. My place is here, and the most noble thing in life is to do this ...' He put his arm round Cleopatra and kissed her.

Cleopatra pulled herself away from him.

'Liar!' she said, and turned to some of the other courtiers. 'Why did Antony marry Fulvia, I wonder, if he didn't love her?' she asked them.

Antony looked at her, smiling. 'For the sake of love, let us not waste our time quarreling. We shouldn't let even a minute of our lives pass without some pleasure. Come, what shall we do this evening?'

'Hear the messengers!'

'Quarrelsome Queen!' Antony had almost shouted at her with impatience, but he quickly stopped himself. 'Now, listen to me. The only messengers I want to hear this evening are the ones you send to me. Then, later on, we will go out and just wander through the streets, and watch the people. Come, my Queen, last night you said that is what you wanted to do.'

Antony took Cleopatra's hand. She saw that he would not bother with the news from Rome that evening, which is exactly what she wanted. Happily she allowed him to lead her out of the room.

Demetrius was amazed at what he had seen and heard. 'Does Antony really think so little of Caesar?' he asked Philo.

'Sometimes he is completely different to the Antony we used to know,' said Philo.

'Well, I am sorry to see it. In Rome people are saying that he has given himself up to the love of this queen. It seems they are right. Let us hope he comes to his senses before much longer.'

## A dangerous woman

Philo and Demetrius had good reason to worry. Antony was no ordinary man, and Rome was no ordinary place.

By the time Julius Caesar died, the Roman world — the Roman Empire as it would soon be known — was already very large. Slowly but surely, Rome's power was spreading further and further, even into the ancient, mysterious land
5  of Egypt. People began to think that the Romans would soon be masters of the whole world.

Although the Romans were strong, they often fought among themselves, and they found it difficult to rule so many different countries and so many different people
10  peacefully. From time to time there were terrible civil wars, when one Roman leader would send his armies against another.

After the death of Julius Caesar, Antony, Lepidus, and the young Octavius Caesar, who was the nephew of Julius,
15  ruled the Roman world together. These three were the most powerful men at the time. So long as they agreed with one another and worked together, the Roman world would enjoy peace. Disagreements, however, were likely to cause terrible trouble.

20  Egypt at this time was still an independent country, but it was slowly falling into the hands of the Romans. The Queen, Cleopatra, was unmarried, and ruled alone. Her great beauty and intelligence were famous throughout the world, and it was said that any man who met her would
25  fall in love with her immediately. Powerful men who fall in love with such a beautiful woman will obey her, and because of that the Romans thought Cleopatra might be dangerous. Antony, therefore had gone to Egypt to meet her and to try to discover if she was plotting against the
30  Romans.

When Antony first saw Cleopatra, she was on a beautiful sailing ship made of gold. The oars were of silver and moved in time to music. The sails were purple and gave out a sweet scent. Cleopatra herself lay on a golden
35  couch. Above her, to protect her from the sun, was a large cloth of gold, and at her side were boys with fans to keep her cool. Antony was overcome by this amazing sight.

Like others before him, he fell in love with Cleopatra when they met face to face.

Cleopatra fell in love with Antony, too. He was as famous for his success in war and his political power as Cleopatra was for her beauty. Cleopatra wanted him to live with her in Egypt for the rest of their lives together.

So Antony stayed in Egypt enjoying the rich, lazy life that Cleopatra and her friends enjoyed. He tried to forget what was happening in Rome and his real purpose in coming to Egypt. 20

## The greatest liar

The news that had come from Rome was very serious. When Antony at last decided to hear the messengers, he was very shocked. He began to realize how weak and stupid he had been. 25

First he heard that Fulvia, his wife, had used her wealth and power to start a war against his brother Lucius. The two had soon made up their quarrel, and then joined forces against Octavius Caesar. In the battle that followed they had lost, and Caesar had forced them to leave Italy. 30 This was very bad news for Antony. He and Octavius Caesar were supposed to be friends, yet Antony's wife and brother had attacked him.

Worse was to come. In the eastern part of the Empire, not far from Egypt, the Persian King had sent armies into 35 the three Roman provinces of Syria, Lydia and Ionia. These were all rich lands controlled by the Romans. Antony had been nearby at the time, but had done nothing to prevent the attack.

5   Last of all, another messenger brought news of the death of Fulvia. After being driven from Italy with Lucius, she had fallen ill and died.

Antony knew that much of this trouble was caused by his own bad behaviour. He was needed in Rome to help
10   fight enemies who were moving ever closer. He decided that he must leave Egypt.

Cleopatra had suspected that something was wrong. 'Antony was quite happy at the beginning of the day,' she told Iras, one of her serving women, 'but suddenly a
15   "Roman" thought struck him, and since then he had been quite serious.'

When Antony hurried into her room, she pretended to be ill.

'I am sorry to have to tell you ...' began Antony. He
20   knew that she would not like what he was going to say.

'Help me, dear Charmian,' Cleopatra cried out. She held on to the arm of her other servant. 'I am feeling faint and shall fall down.' She allowed Charmian to place her on a couch. Slowly she settled down, looking very weak.

25   'Now, my dearest Queen ...' said Antony.

'Please, do not stand so close,' Cleopatra said to Charmian. She pretended she could not breathe easily. She also pretended she was not interested at all in anything Antony had to say.

30   'What is the matter?' Antony was becoming worried.

'Oh, nothing! Take no notice. I can see from the look on your face that you have heard some good news. So? What does your wife have to say? You may go back to her, you know. Truly, I wish she had never let you come!
35   I hope she does not say that I am keeping you here. I have no power over you. You are hers.'

'The gods know best ... ' Antony began importantly.

'Oh, never was a queen so greatly betrayed,' Cleopatra sighed. 'Yet I cannot say I am surprised. Why should I think Antony could be true to me, when he is so false to Fulvia?'

'Most sweet Queen ...'

'No, please. There is no need to make excuses. Just say goodbye, and go. When you prayed to me to allow you to stay, that was the time for words. There was no talk of going away then. Our eyes and lips were all for love, and nothing else. Every part of us was a piece of Heaven. It must still be true, I suppose — or else you, the greatest soldier in the world, have become the greatest liar!'

'What?' Antony was becoming angry.

The two stared at each other for a moment. Then Antony began again. There was no point, he could see, in being gentle. In a plain, simple manner, he quickly told the Queen what he had heard, including the news of the death of his wife, Fulvia. 'Then how false you are! Your wife, whom you love so much, is dead. So where are your tears? Oh, I can see from this how much the news of my own death would affect you!' said Cleopatra.

Antony refused to quarrel. Instead he told her how much he loved her, and that although he had to leave, his heart would always be in Egypt, with her.

## Antony's new wife

Antony's fellow rulers in Rome, Octavius and Lepidus, had been growing angry about Antony's life of pleasure in Egypt. Octavius complained that he was drinking and eating and wasting his time in merry-making while Rome's great enemy, Pompey — the son of the man Julius Caesar had killed, was bringing his army closer.

When Antony reached Rome, he found that his friendship with Octavius and Lepidus had cooled. He felt that he had to do something to regain the respect of his friends, especially Octavius, who was known to be

ambitious and eager to rule Rome alone. And so it was
decided that Antony would marry Octavia, the sister of
Octavius. She was beautiful, noble, and gentle in
character, and not at all proud. She was quite unlike
5   Cleopatra, who thought she was more powerful, and more
beautiful than any other woman alive. In fact, if Antony
had not been in love with Cleopatra, he would have
considered Octavia a perfect wife. The wedding was
arranged for political reasons and it restored the friendship
10   between Antony and Octavius.

When Cleopatra heard that Antony had married again,
she was so angry that she wanted to kill the messenger
who brought the news. However she asked
the messenger some questions about
Octavia's appearance and character.
He replied that Octavia was plain,
short, old, and never had anything
interesting to talk about. Delighted
at this reply, and content that
Antony could not really love
Octavia, Cleopatra rewarded
the messenger with gold.

Although Antony treated his
new wife with great kindness
and respect, he longed to be
back in Egypt with Cleopatra.
A fortune-teller told him that
Octavius would become more
powerful than he, and that he
should return to Egypt, where
he could forget his worries
about Octavius's ambition. He decided to take the fortune-
teller's advice, but before he could leave Rome, he was
called to an important meeting. He, Octavius and Lepidus
35   had to try to persuade Pompey to agree to peace terms.

It was agreed that Pompey would receive Sicily and
Sardinia, two of the Roman lands he had conquered. Both

sides would return their prisoners of war unharmed. At the feast to celebrate the peace agreement, Lepidus behaved foolishly and became drunk. It was clear that he was the weakest of the three rulers of the Roman world.

After the peace agreement, Antony and Octavia left 5 Rome for Athens. Octavius Caesar seemed very unhappy to see them go. In Athens, however, news came that Octavius had gone to war against Pompey again. Moreover, he had spoken insultingly about Antony, in spite of the fact that Antony was now his brother-in-law. 10

Antony sent Octavia back to Rome to talk to her brother. He said that he would gather an army together to make war on Octavius. 'If I lose my honour, I lose myself,' he said. If that happened, it would be better if he were not Octavia's husband. 15

Octavia arrived in Rome, hoping to make peace between her husband and her brother. But when she arrived, Octavius Caesar told her he had received news that Antony had gone back to Cleopatra. He persuaded Octavia that she had been badly treated by Antony and 20 should remain in Rome.

Even though Antony was married to his sister, Octavius still wanted to destroy him. He wanted to be the only ruler of Rome. Lepidus was weak and could easily be removed from power, but to get rid of Antony he would have to 25 make war against him.

## The Battle of Actium

Antony had gathered his army at Actium, which was on the coast, not far from Egypt. He was joined there by Cleopatra. News came that Octavius was approaching 30 Actium with his navy.

Antony's advisers told him that he must not fight at sea. His ships were old and had not been used for a long time, and many of his sailors knew nothing about fighting. Octavius had a new navy, and his men were well-trained. 35

Antony's soldiers could certainly beat the enemy's army, so the best thing would be for Antony to fight Caesar on land.

Antony, however, did not listen to this good advice. He preferred to listen to Cleopatra, who wanted him to fight a sea battle. Antony's navy was defeated and his ships were sunk. This defeat was partly Cleopatra's fault. When she saw that the battle was going badly, she took away her ships and commanded her navy to sail back to Egypt. Antony, having lost everything, told his followers to escape, and followed Cleopatra to Egypt.

Antony felt terrible shame at his defeat, but he still loved Cleopatra and forgave her for her foolish advice and cowardly behaviour. He sent a messenger to Octavius begging to be allowed to remain in Egypt. If that were not possible, then he asked to be allowed to live privately and quietly in Athens. He said that Cleopatra recognized the greatness of Caesar, and asked that her heirs should be permitted to rule Egypt, which was now a Roman possession. Octavius replied that he would not listen to anything Antony asked, but he would respect the wishes of the Queen if she drove Antony out of Egypt or killed him there.

Antony recovered his former courage when he saw how dishonourably Octavius had treated him. He sent a message to Octavius, who by this time had arrived in Egypt with his army. Antony challenged him to a fight, man to man. Octavius refused.

A battle could not be avoided. Octavius was confident that his forces were better than Antony's, and besides, he now had in his army many of Antony's followers. Antony, thinking that he was going to die, said goodbye to Cleopatra and led his army against the forces of Octavius.

To everyone's surprise, Antony's army won the battle. With all his confidence restored, Antony prepared for another battle to drive Octavius out of Egypt. But this battle was fought at sea and, as before, Antony lost.

This was the end of the war between Antony and
Octavius Caesar. Nearly all of Antony's followers had now
gone over to the other side. Antony at last realized he had
lost everything. In despair he blamed Cleopatra. 'She has
betrayed me, that false Queen of Egypt. My love for her      5
has led to my shame and defeat.' His anger made him
mad, and he wanted to kill her. 'The evil creature has sold
me to that schoolboy, Octavius Caesar. The only war left
is the war my heart makes against her. When I have taken
my revenge against her, I shall be finished!'      10

## The death of the lovers

At that moment Cleopatra came along.

'Keep away from me. You just bring me bad luck!' he
shouted at her angrily.

'Why is my lord so angry with his love?' Cleopatra      15
asked, sadly.

'Go away! If not I shall give you what you deserve, and
spoil Caesar's victory march by killing you. Go! Let Caesar
have you! He will put you on show in Rome in front of
the rough common people. He will chain you to his      20
chariot and pull you along behind him, as if you were the
most disgraceful woman in the world. He will treat you
like something in a circus. Then he will allow Octavia to
tear up your face with her fingernails.'

This was too much for Cleopatra. She ran away in terror.      25

But Cleopatra could not change her ways for long. Soon
afterwards she and her two women servants, Charmian
and Iras, hid themselves in the Queen's tomb, where she
would be buried when she died. Cleopatra sent a
messenger to tell Antony that she was already dead. The      30
messenger was to say that the last word the Queen had
spoken was 'Antony'.

Antony, left alone after receiving this dreadful news,
decided that the only honourable thing left for him to do
was to kill himself. But he was afraid. 'I, who once ruled      35

a third of the world with my sword, now have even less courage than a woman. What Cleopatra has done, I must ask someone else to do for me.'

5   He begged his faithful servant to kill him, but the servant, instead of taking Antony's life, killed himself. Seeing that even his servant had more courage than he, Antony fell on his sword. The sword only wounded him and he was too weak to finish the deed properly. He begged some soldiers to put him out of his misery, but
10   they all refused.

Meanwhile, Cleopatra, realizing what Antony might do, sent another messenger, too late, to tell him that she was still alive. Antony was carried, dying from his wound, to the tomb.

15   When she saw him lying at the entrance to the tomb, Cleopatra was filled with sorrow.

'Peace! Peace!' Antony said to her tenderly. 'It was not Caesar's honour that defeated Antony. Antony's own honour caused his death. It is right that only Antony
20   should beat Antony; but how sad it is.

'I am dying, Cleopatra, dying. I cannot cheat death for much longer; just until I lay the last of many thousand kisses on your lips.'

Cleopatra called to her women servants, and the few
25   soldiers who had not run away. They helped Antony inside the monument and laid him down gently. He was very weak. He tried to tell Cleopatra to give in to Caesar and save herself, but she would not listen.

'Do not be sad at the unhappy change that has come
30   upon me at the end of my life,' he said. 'Think of my past fortunes, when I was one of the greatest, noblest princes in the whole world. I do not now die a dishonourable death. I am a Roman, bravely defeated by a Roman. But now my soul is going … I can no more …'

35   'Noblest of men, do you wish to die?' cried Cleopatra. 'Will you not care about me any longer? Shall I live here all alone in this dull world? Without you it is no better

than a pig sty. Oh, see, my women … the crown of this world is melting.'

Antony's eyes closed.

'My lord!'

He was dead.

'Oh, look, how the bright flower of honour dries and drops to the earth. The brave soldier's spear is fallen. Young boys and girls are equal now to men. And there is nothing wonderful left beneath the moon.'

The Queen wept.

Octavius promised Cleopatra that he would treat her well, but warned her that if she, too, took her own life, he would not be so kind to her heirs. But Cleopatra decided that she could not go on living without Antony. She told her servants to bring her crown. And so she prepared for death. On her throat and her arm she placed two snakes whose bites were very poisonous. She was killed instantly and painlessly.

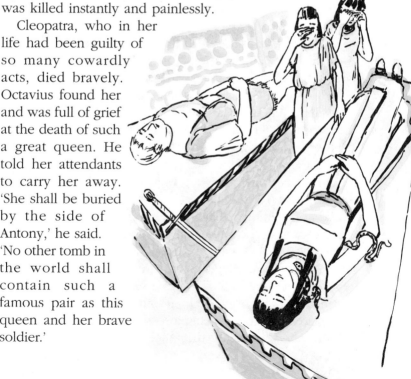

Cleopatra, who in her life had been guilty of so many cowardly acts, died bravely. Octavius found her and was full of grief at the death of such a great queen. He told her attendants to carry her away. 'She shall be buried by the side of Antony,' he said. 'No other tomb in the world shall contain such a famous pair as this queen and her brave soldier.'

# CYMBELINE, KING OF BRITAIN

### The angry king

Cymbeline was King of Britain in the early years of the great Roman Empire. His first wife had died, leaving three young children — two sons and a daughter. The two sons
5 had been stolen when they were very young, and no one had seen them since, so Cymbeline thought of his daughter, Imogen, as his only child.

Cymbeline married again. His second wife was a widow who already had a son named Cloten by her first marriage.
10 She was very cruel to Imogen. She hated the girl because she, and not Cloten, would become the ruler of Britain when Cymbeline died. However, she planned a marriage between them so that when Imogen came to the throne, Cloten would be King.

15 Cloten was a dull, selfish fellow, and Imogen despised and disliked him. Without her father's permission, she secretly married a young man she had known since she was a child. He was Posthumus, a clever young man of fine character, who came from a good family. Before he
20 was born, his father had died fighting for Cymbeline. His mother had died giving birth to him. Posthumus had been brought up in Cymbeline's palace. He and Imogen had often played together when they were children.

The Queen ordered her servants to find out all they
25 could about Imogen. They told her about Imogen's secret marriage, and she immediately reported it to the King. Cymbeline was very angry. Imogen had not asked for his consent to the marriage. Even worse, Posthumus was not a person of royal birth. The King sentenced Posthumus to
30 permanent exile from the kingdom. He must leave Britain and never return. The King also placed his daughter, as a prisoner, in the care of the Queen.

The Queen pretended to be sorry for Imogen because she wanted to win her trust. She hoped to persuade her to give up her marriage to Posthumus and then marry Cloten as she had originally planned. The Queen told Imogen she would permit her to see Posthumus for one last time before he left the country. She urged the two young people to hurry before the King discovered them, but then she went to the King, to make sure that he would find them together.

Posthumus had decided to go to Rome. The lovers said goodbye to each other quickly. Imogen gave her husband a diamond ring and he promised to keep it. On her arm he placed a bracelet as a sign of his love. They promised to be true to each other for life.

At that moment Cymbeline appeared with his lords. Angrily, he ordered Posthumus to leave or be put to death.

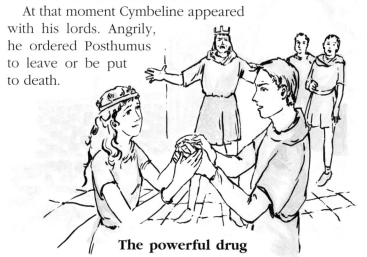

**The powerful drug**

The Queen continued to make plans for her son to become King. She thought she might need to use poison against her enemies, and so she asked the court doctor, Cornelius, to make something for her. Cornelius did not know exactly what the Queen wanted this substance for, but he came to the palace, bringing a small box with him.

'Have you brought the substance I asked for?' the Queen asked when she saw him.

Cornelius handed her the box. 'If you please,' he said, 'I wonder why you have asked me to make such a highly poisonous substance. It will kill anyone who takes it.'

The Queen reminded him that she had been a pupil of his for many years. She had learned much about how to get different substances from plants. She used this knowledge to make perfumes and medicines. She said she just wanted to find out all she could about the substance. She said she would only use it on animals — not on humans.

The doctor did not trust the Queen with such a powerful drug, and he had not given her exactly what she had asked for. The drug in the box would not kill. Instead people who took it would fall into a very deep sleep. They might look dead, but they would wake up again after a while.

The Queen gave the box to a man called Pisanio, who was Imogen's servant and a good friend of Posthumus. The Queen gave it to him as a present. She said that it was a reward for his services. She told Pisanio that the box contained a medicine which would cure all diseases, but in fact she hoped Pisanio would take the drug and die. Then Imogen would have no loyal friend by her side. After that it would be much easier to persuade her to give up Posthumus and marry her son, Cloten.

### Imogen's love is tested

After a long journey, Posthumus arrived in Rome. He soon made many friends there.

One day he found himself in a party of young men, who all came from different countries. They began comparing the beauty and goodness of the ladies of their various homelands. Thinking of Imogen, Posthumus praised her for her character, beauty and loyalty. An Italian named Iachimo asked whether he thought a British lady would be more faithful than any other. They agreed on a

bet about it. Iachimo would go to Britain and try to win
the love of Imogen. If he failed, he would give Posthumus
a large amount of money. If he won, however, Posthumus
would have to give him the diamond ring.

How would Posthumus know what had happened? 5
Iachimo said that if Imogen accepted his love for her, he
would make her give him the bracelet she had promised
to keep. This would prove she had been faithless to
Posthumus.

Iachimo reached Britain and travelled to the court of 10
Cymbeline. He carried a letter with him, written by
Posthumus to Imogen. It said that Iachimo was a friend.
When they met, the first thing Imogen wanted to know
was the news about Posthumus.

'Is my lord well?' she asked. 'Is he in good health?' 15
'Very well, madam.'

'And is he happy? I hope he is.'

'Oh, most happy, madam. What an excellent sense of
humour he has! He's always full of fun.'

'How strange,' said Imogen thoughtfully. 'When he was 20
here, he was often very serious — and no one knew why.'

'Well, madam, he is never serious when he is with us.
He has a friend — a Frenchman, who is serious. This man
spends all his time thinking about some girl in France he
loves. All day long he goes around crying and sighing. 25
Meanwhile the merry Briton (your lord Posthumus)
follows him about, roaring with laughter. "Oh, I will die
laughing," he says, "to think that any man will spend his
free time crying over a woman." '

'Does my lord say such things?' Imogen began to feel 30
hurt.

'Indeed he does. And when those two are together, and
he laughs more than I can tell you.'

In this way Iachimo made Imogen think that her
husband was enjoying himself greatly in Rome, and that 35
he spent little if any of his time thinking about her. Then,
saying how much he admired her beauty, Iachimo tried

to win Imogen's love. However, Imogen was true to
Posthumus, and she refused him.

## An unfaithful wife

When Iachimo saw that she could not be persuaded, he
5  decided to trick her. He asked Imogen if she could keep
his trunk in her bedroom. He told her it was filled with
jewels and other valuable presents for his friends in Italy.
He said it would be much safer in her bedroom, as even
the boldest thief would never dare to go in there. Imogen
10  agreed to have it in her room where it would be safe.

In the evening the trunk was placed in Imogen's room.
Iachimo was hidden in it as part of his plan.

When Imogen was fast asleep, he crept out of the trunk
and looked around him. He looked at all the details of
15  the room and everything in it, remembering each item
very carefully. Softly he removed the bracelet from
Imogen's arm without waking her.
Then he hid in the trunk again.
The next day the trunk
was removed. Iachimo
started his journey back to
Italy, taking the bracelet
with him.

When he arrived in
Rome, he went straight to
see Posthumus. He claimed
he had won his bet and that
Imogen and he were lovers.
Posthumus would not believe
him, but Iachimo described
Imogen's room in detail. He
produced the bracelet which, he
claimed, Imogen had given him.

In this way Iachimo made Posthumus
believe that Imogen was an unfaithful wife.

According to their agreement, Posthumus handed Iachimo
his diamond ring. Bitter at the thought of Imogen's lack
of virtue, he felt that all women were the same. He made
up his mind to hate and curse every one of them.

## Two letters                                                5

Posthumus wrote to his friend Pisanio, Imogen's servant.
He told him about Imogen's unfaithfulness. He wanted
Pisanio to go with Imogen to the port of Milford Haven
on the coast of Britain, and to kill her there. By the same
messenger Posthumus sent a message to Imogen. He said     10
he could no longer live without her and that he was
coming to take her away with him. He begged her to go
with Pisanio to Milford Haven, to wait for him there. He
could not enter Britain, but he would come as far as this
port.                                                         15

When Imogen received this letter, she and Pisanio set
out that very night, for she loved Posthumus dearly. She
had no idea of his desire for revenge on her.

Pisanio felt certain that some 'false Italian' had deceived
Posthumus. He privately decided not to kill Imogen. On    20
the way to the coast, he handed Imogen the letter from
Posthumus. To her sorrow she read, 'Let your own hands
take away her life; I shall give you an opportunity at
Milford Haven; she has my letter for the purpose.' What
had changed his love to hate?                               25

In her grief, life seemed no longer worth living. She
offered her sword to Pisanio and told him to stab her
through the heart with it. Her heart, which used to be so
full of love for Posthumus, was now full of grief.

Pisanio told her he would never carry out Posthumus's    30
order. He comforted her. He suggested that some day she
might find out who had spoken against her to Posthumus.
Then she might be able to prove her innocence.

Imogen wanted to find her husband, to clear up any
misunderstanding and regain his love. She had no desire   35

to return to the palace. Pisanio had an idea. There was a
Roman general at Cymbeline's court named Caius Lucius.
He was due to leave for Italy soon, and would come to
Milford Haven. Imogen could disguise herself as a boy
5  and offer to work for him as a servant. In that way she
could travel to Rome to meet Posthumus.

Imogen quickly agreed, and dressed herself as a boy.
Pisanio said he would go to look for the General. As they
parted, Pisanio gave her the little box which Doctor
10  Cornelius had brought to the Queen. He thought it
contained a wonderful medicine, as the Queen had told
him, and that it might help her in some way.

## The fairy

Pisanio left and went to look for Caius Lucius. Imogen
15  walked towards the coast, but lost her way in a forest.
After two weary days of wandering about, she came to a
cave. No one was there, but she saw food and some
furniture. The cave was someone's home. Being extremely
hungry, she went in, sat down at the table and began to
20  eat some of the food. Then she heard voices.

Three people, an old man and two young men, came
to the cave entrance. They were talking about what they
were going to eat for their supper. The old man looked
in, and saw Imogen there, eating.

25  'Wait, boys,' he whispered to the others. 'Keep still.
There's something in here. If it weren't eating our food, I
would think it was a fairy!'

'What is it, sir?' asked one of the young men. But the
old man could not take his face off the stranger.

30  'I do believe it really is a fairy!' he said. 'Have you ever
seen such beauty in someone no older than a boy!'

Imogen looked up, and was quite frightened at the sight
of three faces staring at her. They looked rough and
dangerous. She thought she was in trouble. She jumped
35  up from the table and away from the entrance.

'Good sirs, please don't hurt me. I shouted to see if there was anyone here before I came in; I was going to beg for what I needed.'

They came closer to her.

She stuck her hand into her purse and took out some coins. 'Look, here's some money for you. I'll pay for the food I have eaten. I was going to leave it on the table before I left, anyway.'    10

'Money, young man?' said one of the two young men, as if he was uncertain what the word meant.

'Dirty rubbish!' shouted the other. 'That's what money is. And so are all those who concern themselves with it. Rubbish!'    15

## Brothers

Imogen was even more frightened. 'Oh, now I have made you angry,' she said weakly. 'But let me just tell you, if you are going to kill me for taking your food, I would have died anyway from not taking it. I have not eaten for    20 days!'

'Where are you going?' asked the first young man roughly.

'Milford Haven.'

'Your name?' demanded the other.    25

'Fidele, sir,' said Imogen, quickly making up a name for herself. 'I was on my way to Milford Haven to meet a relative. Then, almost dead with hunger, I came to your cave. I walked in to get something to eat. I thought no one would mind. I see now how wrong it was ...' Imogen began to cry.

'Oh, never mind; never mind about all that!' the old man interrupted. He pushed the other two out of the way. 'Look, my fine young fellow, you mustn't take us for low, common people. Don't judge us by the look of this rough place we live in. It's good to have you here, really it is. And there's plenty to eat.' He pointed to some large pieces of cold meat on the table and asked her to help herself, which made Imogen cry even more. 'Now, now!' the old man added, taking her arm, 'There will be something much better than that before long. We've been hunting and we have some fresh meat here. We'll be very pleased to have you stay and share our dinner with us. Boys! Come along, now. Make the young man welcome!'

The two young men began to smile at her. Imogen sighed with relief.

'If you were a woman,' said one of the young men, who thought Imogen looked surprisingly beautiful, 'I would want to be your sweetheart.'

'You are very welcome here, Fidele,' said the other, holding out his hand. 'Come along now. Be cheerful, for you are among friends. It's good enough for me that you are a man. I'll love you as my brother.'

## Cymbeline's sons

Although no one realized it at the time, the two younger men were Imogen's long-lost brothers, Guiderius and Arviragus. They had been stolen from Cymbeline's court by the old man, who was one of Cymbeline's lords. His name was Bellarius.

Bellarius had been sent into exile by Cymbeline. He had thought this was very unjust. He had stolen the little boys in order to take his revenge. He had planned to kill them.

However, he found that he could not bear to be so cruel, so he took them to live with him in the forest. He told them his name was Morgan. He did not use their own names, either, but called them Polydore and Cadwal. They grew up to be strong, healthy young men, thinking that Bellarius — or Morgan — was their father. Because of this Imogen had no idea who they really were. 5

Imogen was very tired and she felt quite ill, too. She was glad to be allowed to stay in the cave for a while. She cooked the evening meal, and her cooking skill surprised the three men. Her gentle ways and graceful manners pleased them. She became great friends with the young men during the few days she stayed there. 10

When there was no more food, Bellarius and the two brothers went out to hunt. Imogen, who was still weak from the time she had spent lost in the forest, remained behind. Thoughts of her husband's cruelty and of her own troubles made her unhappy, too. Feeling ill, she took the medicine Pisanio had given her, thinking it would cure her. Immediately she fell into a deep sleep. 15 20

On their return, the brothers found Imogen lying still and lifeless. Arviragus noticed that nothing, not even being touched or moved, would wake her. He thought she was dead. He carried her out to a shady spot in the forest, and laid her on the grass. Then the three men sang funeral songs, and covered her with leaves and flowers. They went away, sorrowing that their new young friend was dead.

When the effect of the medicine wore off, Imogen woke up. She felt quite well. She could not find her way back to the cave and her friends. She began to think it had all been a dream, so wearily she set out for Milford Haven.

<sup>5</sup>

## Imogen joins the army

Meanwhile, strange events were happening. The Roman Emperor had sent his General, Lucius, back to Britain with an army. While Imogen was in the forest, the General and his army were marching through that region on their way to the palace of King Cymbeline.

Posthumus had come to Britain with the Roman army. He still felt that Imogen had been unfaithful to him. He believed Pisanio had carried out his orders to kill her, as he had received a letter from Pisanio which made him think Pisanio had obeyed him. Instead of being pleased, however, he was very sorry for what he had done. He remembered how much he used to love his dear wife.

Posthumus decided that he would leave the Roman army and fight for his own country, Britain, against the Romans. He cared little for his life now. He was ready to die fighting, or be killed by Cymbeline for returning from exile without permission.

Iachimo had come to Britain with the Roman army, too. Imogen, still dressed as a young man, was in the forest when the Roman army marched by. General Lucius found her and took her into his service as an assistant — a page boy.

When Guiderius and Arviragus heard from the soldiers that a battle would soon begin, they set out to join the British army. Bellarius went with them, even though he was quite an old man.

In the great battle that followed, the Britons did badly at first. They were forced to retreat, and for a while Cymbeline's life was in danger. Then the great bravery of Posthumus, old Bellarius and the two brothers, all of

whom fought very hard against the Romans, gave the
Britons time to prepare for another attack. They returned
to the battle and took the Romans by surprise. Finally the
Romans were defeated. General Lucius, the deceitful
Iachimo, and Imogen, still dressed as a boy, were taken          5
prisoner, and brought before the King.

Posthumus had wished to die in battle because of his
grief at Imogen's death. Not finding death, he gave himself
up to Cymbeline's soldiers, who took him to the King. He
was brought before the King at the same time as the three        10
prisoners from the Roman army.

With the King were a number of British lords, Pisanio,
and Bellarius with the two brothers. The Queen and her
son Cloten were not there. They were both dead. Cloten
had been killed in a quarrel. The Queen, failing in her        15
plan to arrange a marriage between Imogen to Cloten, and
feeling guilty about her own wickedness, had fallen sick
and died soon afterwards.

King Cymbeline announced that it was the wish of his
people that the Roman prisoners should be killed. General       20
Lucius begged the King to spare the life of his innocent
young page boy, who was a Briton and, he said, loyal,
obedient, hard-working, and very kind.

## The King finds his children again

Cymbeline looked at Imogen. He did not recognize his           25
daughter, yet he liked the look of the young man. Lucius's
page boy reminded him of someone, though the King was
not sure who it was.

The King said that he would not punish the young man.
In fact he liked him so much that he would give him            30
anything he asked for.

Lucius, who thought his words had saved Imogen, now
expected that Imogen would ask the King to spare his life.
Imogen, however, had a something else in mind. She had
noticed the diamond ring which she had given to              35

Posthumus on Iachimo's finger. She asked the King that Iachimo should be made to tell her everything he knew about how he had got the ring.

Cymbeline said Iachimo must speak the truth. Fearfully, Iachimo told the story of his bet with Posthumus and the cunning way he had won it.

Posthumus heard this confession. At last the truth was clear: Imogen had always been faithful to him. But it was too late to do anything about it now, he thought. He had been the one who had ordered her death. Sick with grief, he stepped before the King. He confessed how, because of Iachimo's lies, he had ordered Pisanio to kill the Princess Imogen. Imogen could no longer bear to see her husband so full of sorrow. She revealed who she really was, turning his grief into joy.

Cymbeline, too, was overjoyed to have his daughter back. In his happiness he approved her marriage, and he freed Posthumus from the sentence of banishment.

There was more joy to come for the old King. Bellarius confessed that the two young men with him were really the King's long-lost sons, Guiderius and Arviragus. Cymbeline who had thought just a short while before this that he had no children at all, now rejoiced at having all three of his children back so unexpectedly. He was so happy that he forgave Bellarius for stealing the boys and welcomed him to his court.

Cymbeline also spared the life of Caius Lucius. With his help, peace was made with the Roman Emperor. The Roman and the British flags once more flew in peace together. Even the false Iachimo went unpunished, since everything had ended so well.

# THE WINTER'S TALE

## The jealous king

Leontes of Sicilia, and Polixenes of Bohemia had grown up together. They had been friends since they were boys. Later, when their fathers died, each became king in his own country. They married, and each had a son, but by that time they were so busy with their kingdoms and their families that they no longer had time to see one another. However, they kept up their friendship through an exchange of letters and presents.

Leontes often invited Polixenes to visit Sicilia and to meet his Queen, Hermione. At last, after many years, Polixenes accepted. He came with his lords and his courtiers, but he left his wife and son at home.

At first the visit was enjoyed by everyone. Queen Hermione had often heard her husband speak about Polixenes, and she grew to like him as much as Leontes did. When the two friends talked about old times, the Queen joined in their laughter.

Some months later, when it was time for Polixenes to return to his kingdom, Leontes urged him to stay. Polixenes replied that he had to attend to some important state business at home. Then Hermione joined her husband in trying to persuade Polixenes to remain with them just a little longer. At her request, Polixenes agreed.

When Leontes saw that, in order to please the Queen, Polixenes had changed his mind and decided to stay, he was not happy. He thought Polixenes was paying too much attention to his wife. He began to notice how much they enjoyed talking together. He began to feel jealous. Soon, like any jealous husband, he started watching his wife for signs that she loved Polixenes.

Hermione, being loyal and loving, did not suspect her husband was growing jealous. She was not as careful as she could have been. She continued to treat her husband's friend with kindness and great affection.

5     Leontes' jealousy grew so much that it changed his character completely. His love for his wife and his liking for his friend quickly turned to anger and hatred. He sent for his most faithful nobleman, Camillo. Saying that his wife now loved Polixenes, he ordered Camillo to poison
10    him. Camillo tried to persuade the King to forget this idea, but nothing he said would change the King's mind. In the end he agreed to carry out the King's orders.

Fortunately Camillo was too kind to do such a terrible thing. He informed Polixenes of the planned poisoning
15    and urged him to leave Sicilia immediately. Of course, Camillo had to leave, too. Leontes would certainly kill him if he remained. Camillo therefore asked Polixenes to let him go with him to Bohemia.

After making their preparations in secret, Polixenes and
20    Camillo sailed away. In his new country, Camillo became adviser to Polixenes, and one of his most trusted friends.

## The Queen's daughter

Leontes grew even more angry when he heard that Polixenes and Camillo had left Sicilia. To him it was a sign
25    that Polixenes was guilty. Since Camillo had gone too, he supposed that he had been helping Polixenes all the time. Leontes went directly to the Queen to accuse her of being in love with Polixenes.

Hermione and her ladies were in the garden, playing
30    with the little prince, Mamillius. At first she thought her husband was joking when she heard what he had to tell her. Then from his appearance and manner, she saw he was serious. Again and again she told him that she was innocent. Leontes would not listen. Hermione was put in
35    prison with one or two ladies of the court to attend her.

Little Mamillius did not understand what had happened, but he longed for his mother, whom he loved dearly. He knew that she was unhappy and in prison. Soon he began to grow thin and weak.

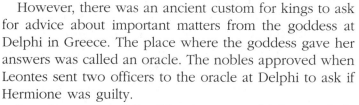

Very few people thought that the Queen was guilty. Her goodness and love for her husband were well known. Several nobles defended her character and begged King Leontes to change his mind. He refused to listen, insisting that they were fools.

However, there was an ancient custom for kings to ask for advice about important matters from the goddess at Delphi in Greece. The place where the goddess gave her answers was called an oracle. The nobles approved when Leontes sent two officers to the oracle at Delphi to ask if Hermione was guilty.

In prison meanwhile, Hermione gave birth to a little girl. The baby was a comfort to her in her sorrow. One day the lady Paulina, one of Hermione's dearest friends, said, 'If you dare trust me with your little girl, I'll show her to the King, and I will ask him to forgive you. Perhaps the sight of the little child will soften his anger.' Hermione consented. Carrying the baby, Paulina went to see the King. She laid the child at his feet.

Bravely Paulina defended the Queen, saying that she was innocent. She begged Leontes to have mercy on his Queen and his little daughter. Leontes refused to accept that the baby was his child, and drove Paulina out of the room.

## A message from the goddess

Antigonus, Paulina's husband, was one of the lords who served Leontes. Leontes accused him of ordering Paulina to bring the baby before him. He told Antigonus to kill
5 the baby immediately. Antigonus said that he would obey any order but that. Leontes then ordered him to sail away with the baby and to leave it in some deserted place, where it might live or die — no one would ever know. If he failed, he and Paulina would be put to death. So
10 Antigonus took the little one away.

After this, news came that the two officers had returned from the oracle at Delphi. Without waiting to receive their message first, Leontes decided to have the Queen tried in a court of his nobles. She was accused of plotting with
15 Camillo and Polixenes against the King, and of helping them to escape by night from Sicilia.

Hermione declared that she, and Polixenes, and Camillo were all innocent. She said that the King's threats did not frighten her, and she was ready to be put to death. Life
20 meant nothing to her without her children and her husband's love. She would accept the answer of the goddess at Delphi, whatever it was.

The messengers arrived at this moment with a letter from the priest at Delphi. 'Open it,' said the King, 'and
25 read what it says.'

The message he heard was this: 'Hermione is innocent; Polixenes blameless; Camillo a loyal subject; Leontes a jealous tyrant; his innocent baby truly his own; and the King shall be without an heir to rule after him if that which
30 is lost is not found.'

## Leontes is sorry

At the news of Hermione's innocence, there was great relief in the whole court. Only the King disbelieved what the oracle had said. He even added that it was false, and
35 had been invented by the Queen's friends. The trial must

continue. As this order was being given, a man hurried in
to say, 'Your son Mamillius, out of grief and shame at the
trial of his mother, is gone.'

'Gone! What do you mean?' said the King.

'He is dead,' replied the messenger. 5

Hermione, hearing this, could bear it no more. She fell
to the ground.

'Carry her away,' replied Leontes, 'her feelings have
overcome her; she will recover.'

But then he began to wonder if he had been wrong all 10
the time. He felt that Hermione must have been overcome
with sorrow for her children, and suddenly his heart was
full of pity for her. 'Care for her tenderly,' he said as she
was carried away, 'bring her back to health again.'

Not long afterwards, Paulina returned. She announced 15
to everyone that something very terrible had happened.
Her anger against the King made her bold.

'Look at what your stupid jealousy has done now!' she
cried angrily. 'Not even a child of nine would believe the
things that you believe. But all your previous foolishness 20
was nothing compared to this latest thing. Your betrayal
of your friend Polixenes, that was nothing; it just showed
what a wretched ungrateful fool you are. And trying to
persuade the honourable Camillo to murder a King —
compared to this, it was just a small fault. Throwing out 25
your baby daughter to die was nothing much either —
though a devil would not be as cruel as you. I do not
blame you even for the death of the prince, whose poor
little heart broke when he saw how badly his foolish father
treated his dear mother. But this latest thing — Oh lords, 30
when I have told you, you will all cry out in sorrow! The
Queen, the Queen, the sweetest, dearest creature, is dead!'

Paulina was so sad and so angry that she did not care
how the King punished her for speaking out. But now
Leontes realized his mistakes. He had only one desire — 35
to set right all the wrong he had done.

'All you have said about me is true!' he exclaimed.

Too late he believed the truth of the letter from Delphi. Its warning made him see that with Mamillius dead, and his baby girl sent to die in some distant land, he had no heir. How he wished his little daughter would come back!
5  Leontes grieved about what he had done for many long years.

## Perdita

Antigonus had already obeyed Leontes' command. He had sailed away and landed on a lonely coast which was part
10  of the kingdom of Bohemia. The captain lowered a boat for Antigonus to take the child to the shore. 'Hurry,' he warned, 'for a bad storm is coming. Don't go far into the forest; there are many wild beasts there.'

Antigonus reached the shore and walked a little way
15  into the forest. He laid the baby down in its royal clothes, and by its side he placed a bundle of clothes and jewels. On its coat he fixed a paper with the name 'Perdita' and a few details of the child's high birth. He hoped that the baby would be rescued and brought up with money from
20  the sale of the gold and jewels.

Antigonus then turned back towards the shore. He never reached the ship, for a bear came out of the forest and attacked and killed him. At almost the same time, the ship was wrecked and the sailors drowned in the great
25  storm that the captain had foreseen.

There were people living not far away from the lonely place where the baby had been left. An old shepherd, searching for two lost sheep, passed that way. With him was a simple youth, who was his son. The youth had been
30  wandering near the shore. He had seen the sinking of the ship in the storm and he had seen the bear attacking a well-dressed gentleman. He told his father about these surprising events.

As they were talking, the shepherd saw a white object
35  beside some bushes. It was the baby. He could see that

it had been left there by someone. The child was richly clothed, so it must have come from a rich family, but there were no wealthy people living in that part of the country. He decided that the child must have been brought in the ship. The man who had been killed by the bear was probably a relation.

The kindly old shepherd lifted the baby up and looked at the treasure in the bundle. 'This,' he thought, 'is a great piece of luck. There is enough gold and silver here to make me a rich man.' He took the baby and the bundle of treasure to his little home. His wife nursed the child tenderly.

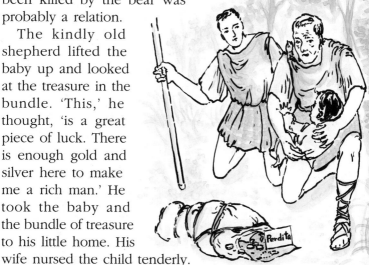

And so Perdita grew up as the shepherd's daughter. With the gold and silver the old shepherd bought sheep and became a wealthy man. But, he told no one where his wealth came from; he feared someone might come to reclaim the child and the jewels.    25

## The shepherd's daughter

In the sixteen years that followed, Perdita grew into a very beautiful young woman, although everyone thought she was just a simple shepherd's daughter.    30

During all that time, Leontes lived alone, sorrowing for the wife and son he had killed, and his lost daughter. He never married again.

Polixenes continued to rule Bohemia. His son, Florizel, grew up to be a handsome and intelligent prince.    35

Camillo remained at the court of Polixenes, and was the King's most trusted adviser, but he longed to return to Sicilia to see his homeland once more.

One day Florizel went out hunting. He was passing the hut of the old shepherd when he saw Perdita. She was only a shepherd's daughter — yet her beauty and grace won his heart. He visited her secretly, not wanting the King to find out about his love.

But the King began to notice that something was wrong. Florizel had stopped doing his work at court, and the King sent his servants to discover why. They reported that Florizel, pretending to be a private gentleman, often visited a shepherd's hut in a distant part of the country. This seemed to be a very strange thing for a prince to do.

Polixenes then sent for his faithful adviser, Camillo. Together they went to the shepherd's home. It was a festival day, a time of fun and dancing. It was the custom for people from near and far to come to the festival, so they went along dressed as two ordinary old men. No one would think it at all strange to see them there.

Great preparations were made by the shepherd and his friends. There was plenty of food and presents of all kinds. The local girls had gathered flowers to give to the guests.

During the festival, Polixenes and Camillo arrived. The Prince, they noticed, was talking to the shepherd's daughter, away from the other people.

The old shepherd welcomed the strangers warmly. He reminded Perdita of her duty as hostess now that his wife was dead. Obediently she approached the two strangers and presented them with flowers. They spoke to her. They listened to her conversation with the Prince. Her speech, her looks and manner did not seem to be those of a girl of low birth. 'All that she says and does seems to be something greater than herself: too noble for her position,' said Polixenes.

While Florizel and Perdita took part in a shepherd's dance, Polixenes asked the shepherd about the 'young man' dancing with his daughter. 'They call him Doricles,' replied the old man. 'He says he is a rich man, and I think he is. He is in love with my daughter. That, too, is easy to see. But if she marries him, she'll bring him more than he dreams of.' He was thinking of some of the jewels he ⁵ had kept hidden away. He planned to give them to Perdita when she married.

## The King's anger

Seeing Florizel and Perdita standing nearby, Polixenes asked him why he had no gifts for his sweetheart on such ¹⁰ a day. He had noticed Florizel bought nothing for her at the festival.

Florizel did not recognize his father. He said he knew that the only gift she wanted lay in his heart. Florizel then took Perdita's hand. With the old stranger watching, he ¹⁵ promised to love no one but Perdita, and to marry her one day. Perdita placed her hand in his to show she accepted him. 'You are a witness to these promises,' Florizel said, turning to the old stranger.

Then Polixenes revealed who he really was. He was angry with his son for daring to offer marriage to a common shepherd's daughter. He ordered them never to see each other again. If they disobeyed him, his son would no longer be Prince, he said, and Perdita and her father would be put to death. With a heavy heart, Polixenes left them.

Camillo remained behind. He hoped to advise Florizel not to anger his father any more. His heart softened towards Perdita, when he saw how gently she spoke and acted.

5 'When the King was angry,' she said, 'I was not much afraid, for once or twice I was about to speak, and tell him plainly, that the same sun that shines upon his court, shines also on our cottage.'

Florizel declared he would not give Perdita up. He 10 would rather lose his claim to the throne. To Camillo he turned for advice, and the old man began to plan how he could help them.

Florizel had a ship not far off. Perdita readily agreed to run away with him and go to another country. The Prince 15 did not wish to live in Bohemia without his Perdita.

Hearing this, Camillo knew what he could do for the lovers and for himself. His old master, King Leontes of Sicilia, had for many years been sorry for his past wrong-doing. Camillo knew Leontes would welcome him back. 20 He could see his old home once again. So he told Florizel, 'If you trust my friendship and advice, let me be your guide. The ship should sail to Sicilia. The King of Sicilia, Leontes, is an old friend of your father. I served Leontes for many years, and know him well. He will receive you 25 very kindly, and he may be able to help you obtain your father's pardon and his consent to your marriage.' Florizel agreed with this plan.

As they all prepared to go on board the ship, the old shepherd joined them. He had heard about where they 30 were going, and planned to show the King of Sicilia Perdita's jewels, which he had kept carefully all this time.

### The Princess

Soon afterwards the little party arrived in Sicilia. King Leontes was told about their landing. He was 35 surprised that no letter from the King of Bohemia had

arrived to announce the visit of his son, the Prince.
However, he received Florizel kindly.

Florizel pretended he was on his way home from Libya.
He said that was where Perdita came from, and he had
married her there. He said his father had asked him to        5
greet his old friend, King Leontes, on the way back. The
rest of his ships had gone ahead with news of his
marriage. That was the reason, he explained, why he had
no followers with him.

At that moment a messenger entered with surprising          10
news. King Polixenes himself had arrived in Sicilia. The
messenger said that Polixenes was looking for his son,
who had run away from Bohemia with a shepherd's
daughter.

From this messenger Florizel learnt that Camillo was        15
already with Polixenes, and, hearing this, he believed
Camillo had betrayed him. But there was more news. Both
Polixenes and Camillo had been seen questioning the
frightened old shepherd. Florizel then confessed to
Leontes that Perdita was not his wife and that he had given    20
him a false story. Leontes went to greet Polixenes.

Florizel need not have worried. Polixenes had set sail
from Bohemia, realizing that Camillo had gone to Sicilia
with his son. He remembered that Camillo wanted to visit
his old country again. So he, too, sailed to Sicilia. To his    25
surprise he found Camillo and the old shepherd waiting
for him. At first Polixenes was very angry with them. He
supposed they had helped his son to disobey him and
escape with Perdita.

But his anger turned to joy at the good news Camillo        30
now gave him. The shepherd had told Camillo how
Perdita, long ago, had been found near the shore. Seeing
the jewels, Camillo suspected that Perdita belonged to a
noble family. The shepherd had found her not long after
Antigonus had sailed with Leontes' baby girl from Sicilia.    35
Moreover, Perdita looked like Queen Hermione! He knew
suddenly who she really was. She was no common

shepherd girl, but Queen Hermione's daughter, whom everyone believed to be dead. Now Polixenes learnt that Perdita, whom his son wished to marry, was his old friend's daughter. She was not a shepherd girl, but a princess.

There was every proof that Perdita was Leontes' daughter. The shepherd had brought the cloak that had been found with the baby. It was the Queen's own cloak. The King recognized the royal jewels. The name 'Perdita' and the letter on the baby's coat were in the handwriting of Antigonus.

When Leontes had first seen Perdita with Florizel, he had been amazed at her likeness to his long-lost queen. Now he was overjoyed at recovering his daughter. He remembered the words of the oracle at Delphi, 'The King shall live without an heir to rule after him, if that which is lost is not found.' His daughter was found. He was delighted that she wanted to marry the son of his old friend, the man he had wronged so many years ago. He welcomed Florizel, Prince of Bohemia, as his son-in-law and heir.

## A very lifelike statue

As Leontes looked at Perdita, he exclaimed at how much she looked like her mother. Then Paulina told the King that she had had a statue made of Queen Hermione. The artist who had made it was very skilful, Paulina said, and the statue looked exactly like Hermione. When he heard this, Leontes wanted very much to see the statue and to show Perdita what her mother had looked like.

Paulina led them to her house where the statue was kept. She drew back the curtains to reveal it. Leontes was speechless with surprise.

'I like your silence,' said Paulina. 'It tells me clearly enough what you think. But speak, my lord, isn't this a good likeness?'

Leontes could almost believe it was Hermione herself. 'That is exactly how she looked,' he said. 'Oh, scold me for my wickedness, dear statue, and then I will say you really are Hermione: although it would be more like Hermione not to scold me, for she was so sweet and full ⁵ of kindness. But there is one thing, Paulina,' he added, 'Hermione did not look as old as this statue suggests.'

'That,' replied Paulina, 'just shows what a skilful man the artist was. He has made her look sixteen years older than when you last saw her. The statue looks like ¹⁰ Hermione now, if she had lived.'

'She might be warm and living now, but instead there is just a cold stone statue — though in those sad days, my heart towards Hermione was even colder and stonier.' Leontes was full of sorrow as he remembered how badly ¹⁵ he had treated his dear wife.

Perdita knelt down in front of the statue and wanted to kiss its hand, but Paulina stopped her, saying that the artist had only just finished his work and the colouring was not yet dry. ²⁰

Leontes was so affected by the sight of the statue that his friends began to feel sorry for him.

'If I had known, my lord, what an effect it would have on you, I would not have shown it to you,' Paulina said. 'If you keep staring at it like that, you will start imagining ²⁵ that it moves.' She went to close the curtains.

'Don't' cried Leontes. 'Let it be. I do believe I can see … The artist must have been amazingly clever! Look, my lord Polixenes. Doesn't it seem to you that it is breathing? And see how cleverly the blue veins in its arm have been ³⁰ painted. They look as if they are actually filled with blood!'

'Then be prepared for something that will surprise you even more,' said Paulina. 'I can make the statue move, and walk about, and take you by the hand. But perhaps you'll think I do this by some kind of witchcraft.' ³⁵

The King answered, 'Whatever you can make her do, I am content to see: whatever she says, I am content to hear. For it must be as easy to make her speak, as it is to make her move.'

Music was heard. At Paulina's order, the statue turned and slowly walked toward Leontes. It opened its arms, and smiled. Hermione — for it was really the Queen — came down and stood in front of her husband.

Leontes felt her arms around him. He knew, then, that it was not a statue, but Hermione herself.

Leontes then learned the truth about what had happened. Sixteen years ago, after Hermione had fainted at her trial and been carried away, Paulina had made a false report of her death. At that time, the Queen could not forgive the King for death of the little Prince, and his cruelty to their baby daughter. She had decided to pretend to be dead.

She had lived in secret with Paulina until, according to the oracle, the lost child had been found. When Perdita was found alive and well, Hermione agreed to return to her husband. Then Paulina had used the idea of the statue as a way of bringing the King and Queen together again after sixteen years.

King Polixenes now joined in the general joy and thanks-giving. Leontes and he were friends once more. The wedding of Perdita and Florizel was celebrated with great rejoicing. Polixenes returned happily to Bohemia. Leontes and Hermione had also found happiness again.

# QUESTIONS AND ACTIVITIES

## CHAPTER 1

*Put these names in the right places:* **Iago, Desdemona, Cassio, Othello, Emilia.**

Othello tried to tell (1) _____ how wicked (2) _____ had been. He said that her husband, (3) _____, knew all about it. He said that (4) _____ had told him (5) _____ had been unfaithful to him, and that she loved (6) _____. Emilia thought (7) _____ was trying to blame (8) _____ for (9) _____'s death, but when he mentioned the handkerchief, she understood at last. She told (10) _____ that she had taken the handkerchief from (11) _____. She said that (12) _____ had asked her to get it for him, though she didn't know why.

## CHAPTER 2(A)

*Put the right information beside each name.*

1  Ventidius  (a) said he was very sad he could not help Timon.

       (b) said he felt insulted because he was asked last.

2  Lucullus   (c) had become very rich.

       (d) said all his money was invested in a business.

3  Lucius    (e) said he had warned Timon not to be so generous.

       (f) said he would have given more than was asked.

4  Sempronius  (g) said it was a bad time to lend money.

       (h) had never repaid any of his debts to Timon.

## CHAPTER 2(B)

*What should these words say?*

Timon gave gold to Alcibiades in order to bring (1) **syrime** and ruin to the people of Athens. He thought Apemantus was a (2) **adcrow** for pretending to be a friend to those he could not (3) **scepert.** He refused to return to the company of those he hated and (4) **oscrend.** He gave gold to the thieves and (5) **supeddare** them to continue stealing. He would not let his (6) **wradest** serve and (7) **fromoct** him. He refused to lead the (8) **scizient** of Athens in their (9) **glurgest** against Alcibiades.

## CHAPTER 3

*Put the ends of the sentences in the right places.*

(a)  hated having to win the approval of the people.
(b)  could not refuse when his mother asked him to make peace.
(c)  called them dogs and blamed them for being so stupid.
(d)  said the honour of serving Rome was enough for him.
(e)  insulted the people and the tribunes in public.

The Romans captured Corioli and offered Caius Martius most of the property that had been taken. Caius Martius (1) _____. For this, the Romans called him Coriolanus.

The people agreed Caius Martius had done much for Rome. However, Caius Martius (2) _____. He said rough people needed to be ruled firmly.

Cominius suggested that Coriolanus should become a consul. However, Coriolanus (3) _____. He did not want to make a speech in the market place.

Coriolanus became angry when one of the tribunes called him a traitor. He (4) _____. By doing this he broke the law of Rome, and he was sent into exile.

Coriolanus met Aufidius and said he would join him in his war against Rome. However, later he (5) _____. Because of this the Volscians killed him, thinking he was a traitor.

## CHAPTER 4(A)

*Put the words of Brutus's thoughts in the right order.*

1 Caesar would be [danger] [state] [to] [a] [the].
2 Caesar might take away [of] [people] [the] [the] [rights].
3 Caesar had seemed sad [when] [crown] [refused] [the] [he].
4 He might accept the crown if [changed] [their] [people] [the] [minds].
5 After that everyone [obey] [would] [to] [him] [have].
6 They [their] [would] [freedom] [lose] [all].
7 The only way to prevent this [killing] [Caesar] [by] [Julius] [was].

## CHAPTER 4(B)

*Choose the best answers.*

1 What did Casca think about the storm? (a) It had no special meaning. (b) It reminded him of an ordinary man whose power had become enormous. (c) Something awful was going to happen.

2 Caesar went to the Capitol in the Ides of March because (a) Calpurnia had dreamed about what would happen; (b) the Senate had decided to offer him the crown; (c) a fortune-teller had said he should be careful on that day.

3 Brutus killed Caesar because (a) Brutus thought his duty to Rome was more important than friendship; (b) he secretly hated Caesar; (c) he did not want to share his secret with his wife, Portia.

4 How did Antony make the crowd in the Forum angry? (a) By talking about the importance of freedom. (b) By telling them that Brutus was an honourable man. (c) By telling them about the contents of Caesar's will.

## CHAPTER 5

*Put the words in the right gaps to say what this part of the story is about:* **pieces, provinces, dangerous, ill, famous, plotting, forces, behaviour, news, closer, face, fighting, political, trouble.**

The Romans thought Cleopatra, the Queen of Egypt, might be (1) _____, so Antony went to try to discover if she was (2) _____ against the Romans. He fell in love with Cleopatra when they met face to (3) _____. Cleopatra fell in love with him too, for Antony was (4) _____ for his success in war and his (5) _____ power. Antony loved Cleopatra so much that said he didn't care if the Roman world fell to (6) _____.

Antony received (7) _____ that his wife, Fulvia, had joined (8) _____ with his brother, Lucius, and that they had been (9) _____ against Octavius Caesar. Also, the Persian king had attacked three Roman (10) _____, and that Fulvia, forced to leave Italy with Lucius, had fallen (11) _____ and died. Antony knew that much of the (12) _____ was caused by his own bad (13) _____. He was needed in Rome to help fight enemies who were moving ever (14) _____. He decided that he must leave Egypt.

## CHAPTER 6

*Put the right names in the right places. Choose from* **Iachimo, Posthumus** *or* **Imogen**.

Iachimo and Posthumus made a bet about whether British ladies were faithful to their husbands. They agreed that (1) _____ would go to Britain to try to win the love of (2) _____. If (3) _____ accepted his love, (4) _____ would make her give him the bracelet that (5) _____ had given her. When (6) _____ returned to Rome, the bracelet would prove to (7) _____ that (8) _____ had been an unfaithful wife. If (9) _____ succeeded, (10) _____ would give (11) _____ the ring that (12) _____ had given him.

## Chapter 7(A)

*Put the descriptions with the right names.*

| | | | |
|---|---|---|---|
| 1 | Leontes | (a) | trusted adviser of Polixenes |
| 2 | Hermione | (b) | lover of Florizel |
| 3 | Polixenes | (c) | Hermione's husband |
| 4 | Camillo | (d) | dear friend of Hermione |
| 5 | Florizel | (e) | mother of Perdita |
| 6 | Paulina | (f) | son of the King of Bohemia |
| 7 | Antigones | (g) | King of Bohemia |
| 8 | Perdita | (h) | husband of Paulina |

## Chapter 7(B)

*Put these sentences in the right order.*

1 In fact Hermione had decided to hide from Leontes and live quietly with Paulina until her little daughter was found.
2 In that way the King and Queen of Sicilia were reunited after so many years.
3 At the trial, Hermione became ill when she heard that little Mamillius had died, and she fainted.
4 When Perdita returned to Sicilia with Florizel, it was time for Hermione to reappear.
5 Paulina took her away, and then returned to the palace to tell the King that Hermione was dead.
6 Paulina arranged for Hermione to look like a statue, and then she brought Leontes to see her.

## GRADE 1

Al

Le

Th

C

Jack London

**Emma**
Jane Austen

**Jane Eyre**
Charlotte Brontë

**Little Women**
Louisa M. Alcott

**The Lost Umbrella of Kim
Chu**
Eleanor Estes

**Tales From the Arabian
Nights**
Edited by David Foulds

**Treasure Island**
Robert Louis Stevenson

**and Other**

O. Henry

**Lord Jim**
Joseph Conrad

**A Midsummer Night's Dream
and Other Stories from
Shakespeare's Plays**
Edited by David Foulds

**Oliver Twist**
Charles Dickens

**The Talking Tree and Other
Stories**
David McRobbie

**Through the Looking Glass**
Lewis Carroll

**The Stone Junk and Other
Stories**
D.H. Howe

## GRADE 2

**The Adventures of Sherlock
Holmes**
Sir Arthur Conan Doyle

**A Christmas Carol**
Charles Dickens

**The Dagger and Wings and
Other Father Brown Stories**
G.K. Chesterton

**The Flying Heads and Other
Strange Stories**
Edited by David Foulds

**The Golden Touch and
Other Stories**
Edited by David Foulds

**Gulliver's Travels —
A Voyage to Lilliput**
Jonathan Swift

## GRADE 3

**The Adventures of Tom
Sawyer**
Mark Twain

**Around the World in Eighty
Days**
Jules Verne

**The Canterville Ghost and
Other Stories**
Oscar Wilde

**David Copperfield**
Charles Dickens

**Fog and Other Stories**
Bill Lowe

**Further Adventures of
Sherlock Holmes**
Sir Arthur Conan Doyle